A Kingdom
of Blood and
Betrayal

A Kingdom of Blood and Betrayal

USA TODAY BESTSELLING AUTHOR

HOLLY RENEE

Visit my website at www.authorhollyrenee.com.

Cover Design: Forensics and Flowers

Editing Team: Brittni Van of Overbooked Author Services, Cynthia Rodriguez of The Beta Bruja, Ellie McLove of My Brother's Editor, Tori Ellis, Lo Morales, and Rumi Khan.

AUTHOR'S NOTE

A Kingdom of Blood and Betrayal should only be read by mature readers (18+) and contains scenes that may make some readers uncomfortable.

This book contains depiction of sexually explicit scenes, violence, assault, and sexual assault. It contains mature language, themes, and content that may not be suitable for all readers. Reader discretion is advised.

For Audrina—
I love you, little one.

ONE

I hated him.

It was the only truth I could cling to because I was unsure of everything else.

I hated him for making me trust him when I shouldn't have. I loathed him for making me see a future that was nothing more than a deception.

He was no better than his brother. At least Gavril had the decency to show me who he really was. He took from me, but not in the same way Evren had. Evren had made me want him, beg for him, and it was nothing more than a manipulation.

I fell for him when I wasn't supposed to, and he had let me fall.

He was the heir to the Blood kingdom, everything I had been taught to fear, and he had let me fall.

I stared at his back as he started to set up the tent. I was surrounded by my enemies, but all I could look at was him. His gaze landed on me, and I forced myself to look away. I refused to meet his eyes. Instead, I stared ahead and watched his mother as she spoke softly to one of her guards. The guard that had been ready to hurt her son only hours before.

She was so different than what I expected the Blood queen to be. She was softer than the legends that were told of her. The way she continuously pushed her hair out of her face as she helped her men set up camp reminded me of my mother. My chest ached as I thought of her; after all, she was the one who had so easily handed me over to people who were only planning to use me.

She had sealed my fate as easily as the star marks on my skin.

Evren's magic caressed my skin like a whisper, but I refused to acknowledge it. He hadn't let it fall from me since we left the forest edge en route to the Blood Court. He hadn't refused me my own horse, not after I absolutely declined to go anywhere near him, but he *did* refuse to give me space. He kept his dark magic wrapped around me for the duration of the ride. It moved and embraced me as if it was checking to make sure I was all right.

But I wasn't. How could I be?

I tried to garner up my own power to blast his touch away from me, but I was tired. Far too tired, and I didn't know how to control my magic like he did. Magic that I didn't understand, that I hadn't even known I had.

Magic that felt so familiar even though we had just met.

I thought back to a time before Evren, when I had been alone with my mother in our village. Had my magic been with me all along even then? Had my mother known? Had my father?

I could still feel it coursing under my skin. My magic had been awoken inside me, and I wasn't sure how I had never noticed it before. It felt wild and reckless, like an extension of me I'd yet to meet.

"Princess," Evren whispered his name for me, and my gaze slammed into his. It was on the tip of my tongue to tell him not to call me that, but I didn't say a word. I just stared up at him and prayed that he could see the anger writhing inside me. "You need to get some rest. We'll reach the Blood Court by morning."

I tried to ignore the noise from the Blood soldiers that surrounded us. They were all watching me carefully even though they had given me a wide berth. They didn't trust me, and I didn't trust them.

I trusted no one. Not anymore.

I pushed off the tree I was leaning against and moved toward the tent. He held the flap open for me, and I passed by him quickly, careful not to let his skin touch mine. But gods, I could feel him. Every part of my body felt on edge where his magic was touching me, my marks dying for more, but I held it all in.

I would never allow the heartless prince to touch me again. It didn't matter that my body craved him.

He was my enemy and my betrayer. I had no business feeling comfortable in his presence or beneath his touch, but I couldn't explain it. His magic infuriated me, but the way it swirled around me made my marks feel alive and my magic thrum.

He was my enemy, but he was also my mate.

He followed me into the tent, and my spine stiffened as I turned to him. There were two bedrolls on the cold, hard ground.

"You are not staying in here with me."

Evren ignored my words and moved toward one of the rolls. He groaned as he sat, and I could see the exhaustion on his face. My fingers ached to reach forward and run my thumb over the deep crease between his eyes. Even through my anger, my chest felt heavy as I watched him.

"I am." His magic tightened around me almost unnoticeably as he started pulling off his boots.

"Then I will sleep somewhere else." I moved toward the tent opening, but his magic hardened, holding me in place. No matter how hard I tried, he still held me captive in both body and mind.

"You're crazy if you think that I will allow you out of my sight for even a moment."

"Because I'm your prisoner?"

"Because you're my mate." He set his boots to the side and braced his arms on his knees as he stared up at me. "You can hate me all you want, princess, but that fact is still true."

I knew he was right. I could feel the truth of his words all the way to my bones, but I refused to accept it. He was supposed to be more, and he proved to be everything I had feared.

And I wasn't going to be tied to him because fate deemed it so. I was tired of relying on fate and the life she had cruelly handed me.

"I am not your mate."

Evren clenched his jaw as he stared up at me, and I could see the fury in his eyes. *Good.* I was furious too.

"You're not leaving this tent, princess."

"Says the adoring mate." I crossed my arms as I looked at him. "Did you take lessons from your brother?"

"I am not him, Adara," he snapped, his voice shaking with his anger.

"No." I shook my head as emotion clogged my throat. I could feel moisture pooling in my eyes and that only made my own anger flare. "You're worse."

His knuckles turned white as he clenched his fists. "What would you prefer? Would you like for me to let you go out into that camp with men who were just so willing to take you from me? Would you prefer that I let your fate be up to them?"

My pulse hammered in my chest as I thought about what he was saying. "Doesn't that bother you?" I watched him carefully for anything that would clue me into what he was thinking. "You are their prince, but they were more than willing to rip me from your fingers."

"My mother is their queen." He pushed his hand through his hair in frustration, but I couldn't take my eyes off of him. "And I lost sight of my role."

I could feel his anger thrumming through his magic. Fear and anticipation spiked through me as it traced over my skin.

"And what is your role, Evren?"

"I was always meant to get you away from him." He shook his head in frustration. "But not until he was weaker. Not until I could do so without him knowing it was me."

"So, what? You were just biding your time as the dutiful brother and son until you could rip everything out from under them?"

Evren stood and moved toward me, and I took a step back against the edge of the tent as his voice snapped. "What I did, princess, was everything that I could to protect my people. You can say I'm as bad as Gavril all you want, but you know nothing of his cruelty."

His words ricocheted through me and settled deep in my gut. He was right. I knew little of Gavril or what he was capable of, but I was still angry. I still wanted a fight because his words were a reminder that I knew little of him as well.

"And the way you fucked me? Was that for your people, prince? Was that to protect me from his cruelty?"

He narrowed his eyes as he searched my face, and he lifted his dark, magic-stained fingers until they wrapped around the back of my neck and forced me to look up at him. "When I *fucked* you, that was for no one other than you and me." He moved closer still, his breath leaving a trail of chill bumps against my neck. "You make me greedy." His lips whispered over my jawline, and I couldn't contain the small moan that fell from my lips. "You make me want to forget any duties that I have and just get lost in you for eternity."

"That will never happen again." My voice lacked strength, and I hated that Evren could recognize my weakness. I could feel his smile as he grazed his lips against my ear.

"We both know that's a fucking lie, princess," he purred.

"You want me just as badly now as you did before you saved me with your magic."

"I don't want you." I shook my head even as pressure built between my thighs. Being this close to him was bad for my head. The smell of him overwhelmed me. The feel of his magic flooded my senses. There was a familiarity that made my marks buzz along my skin, but his magic also felt like phantom hands that were trying to discover every inch of me.

It was hard to remember why I hated him when he was near. It was hard not to reach out and move into the small space he had left between us.

"You may not want me, but gods, I want you. I love fucking you." His nose ran along my jaw, and he inhaled a sharp breath. "It makes me so fucking hard to carry your scent on my body and to know that every male around me knows that you belong to me."

My stomach tightened at his words, and I tried to swallow down my need for him as I continued to shake my head softly.

I didn't belong to him.

I never had. Not really.

But every part of me was begging me to let his words be true. I couldn't see his betrayal when he was choking me with desire. I would suffocate on it, and he would make me thank him for it with my last breath.

My fingers trembled as I raised them and pushed against his chest. I needed space.

Space he wasn't willing to give me.

"Don't push me away, princess." His words were soft and vulnerable as his hands grabbed mine and pushed until my fingers dug into his chest. They were branding his skin, almost to the point of pain, but I could hardly notice when he was staring down at me like he was. "Don't hate me for the choices I've been forced to make."

I jerked my hands away from him as reality set in. I could

still remember the way his face had looked when I realized who he was. I could still taste the way my own magic had become bitter against my tongue.

I moved past him, toward the bedroll he had laid out for me, and I pulled it to the far edge of the tent. "Don't delude yourself into thinking that I will fall to my knees before you simply because you wish it so. No one held a dagger to your neck and made you deceive me. No one made you pretend to be something more with me in the name of saving your people. You want to pretend to be a savior, Evren, but you are just as much a villain as your brother."

"Is that what you want me to be?" He watched me as I dropped onto my bedroll and lay against the rough fabric. "You want me to be the man that you hate?"

"I didn't realize you were giving me a choice."

"We all have choices, princess, but there aren't always two clear paths to choose from. Do you think I knew I was going to end up hurting you? Do you think I had any fucking clue that I was going to find my mate in the girl who is meant to change our world?"

I stared up at him, but I didn't say a word.

"You have a choice to make too. You can go back to him if that's what you choose. You can lie down and become what-ever he wishes to make you." His fists clenched at his sides. "Or you can stay here with me. You can stay here with your mate."

"Those are my two choices?" I wrapped my arms around my chest and stared at the wall of the tent. "Stay with your evil brother or stay with the man who made me believe—"

"Made you believe what?" He ran his hand over his jaw as he stared down at me. "I may be the son of the Blood queen, but that doesn't make me any less of the man you wanted. I have an entire kingdom to think about. There are far too many people counting on me for me to forget everything because I found my mate. But it doesn't make what has happened between us any less real."

"Prince Evren," a gruff voice called his name from the front of the tent, and we both tensed. I had forgotten about everyone but him. I hadn't even thought of the others hearing.

I could hear them now, moving around the camp, and I wondered what they thought of me.

"Get some rest. I will be back shortly to check on you."

"Don't." I shook my head as I lay down and turned my back to him. *Please don't.*

He left the tent without another word, and I clamped my eyes shut and prayed for sleep to claim me.

TWO

I shot up and reached for my dagger as my heart lodged in my throat. Except it wasn't there. *Shit.*

I was in a camp full of vampyres, full of my enemies, and I had no way to protect myself. I searched through the dark tent as the sound of groaning filled the small space. I couldn't tell if it was coming from inside the tent or outside, but I knew it was Evren. I knew it without a doubt, and I jumped to my feet as his ragged breathing racketed up the beating of my heart.

I crept toward the opening of the tent and tried to pull my power forward. For the first time since I thought Queen Veda's men were going to hurt Evren, I could feel it coursing through me, snaking through my veins like it was awaiting my word.

My hand wrapped around the thick material of the tent flap, and I was just about to open it, when I heard his groan from behind me. I spun around and blinked, begging my eyes to adjust to the dark, and then I saw him.

Evren was lying on his bedroll on the opposite side of the tent from where I had been, and he was alone. I stepped closer as I breathed a sigh of relief that no one was with him, that no one was hurting him. I took a step toward him, and another groan fell from his lips. His fists were clenched into his bedroll as his neck bowed from the ground, and he was in pain.

"Evren," I whispered his name, but it was no use. He couldn't hear me. He couldn't hear anything through his agony. I rushed toward him and fell to my knees at his side, but I was fearful to touch him. Fearful to rouse him when he looked so far gone from this world. "Evren, please."

"No." The word was ground out through his teeth, and a deep ache shot through my chest as I watched him. I had never seen him like this, never considered what he had been through.

"Evren." I reached forward and shook his arm, but he jerked it out of my touch. His face grimaced as if my touch had burned him.

My magic swirled through me, and even though I had no idea what I was doing, I reached inside of me and let it fall from my fingers in a desperate plea. *Help him,* I silently begged my magic as the inky black smoke swarmed the tent.

It seemed to obey, to calm under my command, and the swirls of darkness found Evren and Evren alone. It brushed against his skin, not leaving a single inch untouched, and I watched as the deep crease between his brows slowly smoothed away. His hands relaxed and his breathing evened, and just when I thought that I had fully calmed him, my name fell from his lips. He shot up in his bedroll, and his hand found his dagger before I had a single moment to react. But my magic wrapped around his wrist before he could lift it in my direction.

"Princess?" He said my name with confusion coating the word, and I tried to pull my magic back into me.

But it wouldn't come.

"I'm sorry." I looked up to meet his dark eyes before quickly looking away. "You were having a nightmare."

"Shit," he cursed under his breath before he searched my gaze with panic flooding his. "I didn't mean to wake you."

"Are you okay?" I shouldn't have cared. I shouldn't have

been forcing my hands to stay still so they wouldn't reach out and trace every inch of his skin until I was certain he wasn't hurt.

He didn't deserve those things from me.

"Yes." He nodded his head, but he didn't seem sure. He started to lift his hand, but my magic held it in place. Not as a restraint but as if it was desperate to not let him go. "Your magic." He moved his fingers through the smoke, and I felt the motion as if he was stroking my spine.

"I can't control it," I whispered the words I hated with a voice that showed how much he affected me. I didn't want to be weak, and I desperately didn't want to show my weakness to him.

Because I didn't trust him to not use it against me.

"Yes, you can." He nodded and leaned forward until his chest was completely wrapped in my magic. "You are its master, princess. Call it back into you. Make it bow to your will."

I focused on what he was saying, but my heart was still racing and my skin felt alive from where my magic touched his skin. I couldn't concentrate on anything other than him.

Evren reached forward, and I flinched away from his touch. It didn't matter how affected I was by him; I didn't want to be the stupid girl who simply allowed him to lead me to slaughter. He was my enemy now more than ever, and I needed to remember that.

"Let me help you, Adara." He pressed his hand against my chest firmly, and I felt it ground me to my core. "Feel it here." He pressed harder, and I took in a ragged breath. "Call it from here."

I didn't understand what he meant, but I tried to concentrate on that spot where his hand was touching. I focused on it and it alone, and I clamped my eyes closed as my chest rose and fell beneath his touch.

Come back to me.

I felt my magic pause as if it heard me. It hesitated as it

rolled through the tent, and I called it again as I felt the weight of it bearing down on me.

Come back to me.

This time it listened.

Slowly, it seeped back toward me, and I allowed it to do so. I breathed it in, desperate to feel it back inside me.

With every inch that sank back into me, I felt more complete. It snaked its way back into my veins, and I could taste my own power as it did so.

"That's it. Let it come to you." His words fell over me as my magic filled me, and I slowly blinked my eyes open to look at him.

His hand was still on my chest, and his thumb slowly stroked over the base of my neck as the last of my magic disappeared inside me.

We were silent for a long moment as we simply stared at one another. There were so many thoughts running through my head, so many words I was desperate to whisper from my lips, but I would have been foolish to say any of them.

"I should go back to my bed." My voice trembled.

"You should stay." His dark eyes were pleading, and I hated how badly I wanted to soothe that look on his face.

"We both know that I shouldn't," I spoke softly as I shook my head.

"Stay."

I looked at him like he had lost his mind. I wasn't his to command. I didn't answer to the man who betrayed me beyond all others, but still something inside me begged me to listen to him.

"I hate you."

His eyes shuttered, but he simply nodded. "I know you do, but you can hate me tomorrow. For tonight, just stay."

I pushed up off my knees as I shook my head. I avoided looking at him as I climbed to my feet because I knew I needed to put distance between us. I hated him, but my body still called to him as if it couldn't imagine leaving his side. But before I could move away, he caught my hand in his and clung to me with a heartbreaking desperation.

He pressed my palm to his chest, and his heart raged beneath my fingertips.

"Please just stay for tonight. Just tonight." His hand trembled against my own, and I bit down on my lip as my chest seemed to ascend and descend to the same frantic beat. "Please, Adara. I need you."

His words sliced through me, cutting through every bit of resolve I had left, and I knew that I would end up letting this man destroy me if he asked me to. He had shown me exactly who he was, but I was still willing to walk into the fire as if he hadn't.

I looked back to my bedroll as I tried to fight the urge to say yes. I felt weak giving in to him. It was sickening how hard it was to push the word no from my lips.

"Just tonight." My lips trembled as I said the words, but his hand steadied against mine. He pulled me forward until I had no choice but to drop back to my knees in front of him. He lifted my hand in his, and I couldn't look away as he brought my wrist to his mouth and pressed a gentle kiss to the sensitive skin on the inside.

The same skin his brother had torn open with his dagger and taken from. The same skin that I thought he had healed.

I attempted to pull out of his touch, but he held firm, dragging me closer to him inch by inch. Just as our chests were about to meet, Evren laid back and pulled me down with him. We were hardly touching, only his hand still on my wrist, but I could feel him everywhere as I lay at his side and stared into his handsome face.

He wasn't saying anything. Just silently watching me with

his hand in mine, and I didn't understand how he was so calm when I felt like screaming.

"What were you dreaming about?" The question slipped through my lips before I could think better of it, and I watched the edge of pain that still filled his eyes.

"You." His gaze searched over my face as I flinched back from his answer.

"Me?"

"Yes." He nodded before lifting his hand and sliding two fingers across my cheek until he tucked a stray piece of hair behind my ear. "I dreamed of what I have to lose, princess. I dreamed of what my brother would be willing to kill for."

A chill ran down my mark, and I swallowed down my fear at the truth of his words. Gavril would kill to get me back, but how far would he go? Would he hurt Evren in order to get the power that flowed through my blood?

"He is your brother." The words slipped past my lips and my chest ached for him. It was something both Evren and I shared. Those who were our own blood, the people who should have cared for us most, were more than willing to use us so easily.

"He is." Evren looked down at my wrist, and I wondered if he could remember the night we left as easily as I could. Did that night haunt his dreams as it did my own? "But that doesn't mean anything, Adara." His thumb traced over my scar before he slowly looked back up at me. "He will stop at nothing until he has you back."

"I won't go back."

His grip tightened on my wrist. "I know. I won't let him take you again."

"And if that means he tries to kill you to get to me?"

"You are mine, consequences be damned."

"Yet you would so willingly use me as a pawn in your games?" These were games of kingdoms. A game I had no business being part of.

"Is that what you think I'm doing?" He didn't speak a single word that lacked conviction. "Do you not think it would be far easier for me to give in to what my father wants or even my mother? Do you honestly think I wanted to fall for the one person I shouldn't want, the one person who could destroy everything?"

I didn't say a word in return. I simply stared up at the tent ceiling as I tried not to let his words affect me. I was failing miserably, and I feared he could hear the erratic beat of my heart.

"I have spent my entire life making decisions based on others, princess. If I was thinking of no one other than myself, then I would have stolen you away the first moment I had the chance. I would have stolen you away and never looked back."

"Your mother?" I was desperate to know how many of his decisions had been affected by her. What would his mother have him do with me if he allowed her the chance?

"My mother, my kingdom, my friends." He tucked his arm behind his head and rolled to his back. He stared up at the tent ceiling too, and I wondered what thoughts were running through his head that he didn't say aloud. "The acts of my father, and my brother after him, have determined the fate of my decisions more than anything. It is often that we are ruled by hate far more than we are ever controlled by love."

Chill bumps ghosted over my skin. He was right. Far too many of my own decisions were fueled by hate. Hate for my mother and the decisions she made. Hate for his family for the life they forced me to live. Hate for the dreams that plagued my mind of my father, whom I didn't even know.

"But your powers are…" I trailed off, and he turned to look at me.

"I'm strong, Adara." He lifted his fingers just above his chest and let his magic fall from them. It coiled around his wrist almost as if it were alive and eager to touch him. "But I am not strong enough to defeat them. Not on my own."

"But you're strong enough with me?" Fear consumed me, but I didn't know what I feared the most. The fact that I was going to be used in this war against kingdoms or the fear I wouldn't be what they had expected of me.

That everything that had happened wouldn't be worth it.

"It's not about me being strong enough." He finally looked over at me, and there was something in his gaze that I couldn't place. "It's about what we become together. It's about the choices we'll make as mates."

"And what if that's not what I want? What if I don't choose to be everything that the world has deemed me to be?"

"I fear you don't have a choice in that. Neither of us do." He didn't take his gaze off me as he lifted his hand and pressed his fingers to my cheek. "But if I did have a choice, Adara, I would choose you."

I shook my head as I watched him because I couldn't allow myself to believe his words. Believing them made me weak, they made me vulnerable to being hurt even more than I already was.

"I would choose you over anything, princess."

He leaned forward and closed the space between us, and I didn't stop him. I simply let my eyes fall closed as he pressed his mouth to mine and kissed me with desperation that was far too familiar to my own.

His kiss felt like a brand. It felt like an apology that he would never be able to say with his words.

And I chased the feeling of it. I kissed back just as hard, and I moaned into his mouth when his hand grazed over my neck. I wanted him.

I wanted his body, his passion. I wanted him to make me forget everything but this moment we were in.

I wanted to forget that I was the Starblessed and he was the prince of both blood and magic. We were mates, and I wanted to think of nothing else in that moment.

But he slowed the kiss, and reality crept its way back in. He pulled away from me slightly before pressing another gentle kiss to my mouth.

He searched my face, and there was so much indecision staring back at me in his own.

"We should sleep, princess." He ran his fingers along my cheeks, and I could see him warring with himself. "Tomorrow will bring much for us to face."

I clamped my eyes shut as he guided me until my head was laying against his chest.

I felt his next words rumble beneath me. "But we will face them together."

THREE

The warmth of the sun was bleeding through the tent, and I moaned at the delicious way it heated my skin. I could stay in this moment forever with my eyes still closed and the kiss of the morning welcoming me. Nothing could touch me there. Not the truth of what the day was to bring. Not the heartbreak that still lay dormant in my chest.

It was just me and the fantasy that my slumber allowed.

I reached to my side, my body craving more warmth than even the sun could provide, and my hand was left wanting. I blinked my eyes open against the brightness that filled the tent and reality came crashing in.

I was still a prisoner to those outside the tent, and I was alone.

Voices were calling orders to one another outside, but I didn't care about any of them. Evren was gone.

I stayed with him last night when he asked me to, and now, I knew I should have felt relieved that he was gone when I awoke, but I felt foolish.

I threw the small blanket off me and moved back to the side of the tent where my bedroll still laid on the grass. I quickly slipped my boots onto my feet and rolled up my bedding with short, frustrated movements.

I put together Evren's bedroll as well because I couldn't stand to look at it any longer. I dropped both by the door of the tent before I took a deep breath and pushed my hair out of my face.

I stepped out of the tent and tried to leave every bit of my insecurities behind me. I was in a camp full of my enemies without my dagger, and I wouldn't allow them to see that their prince had given me every reason not to trust him, yet I had still given him more of myself than I should have allowed. I was foolish enough to only allow one of them that pleasure, and even though he had already proven what he was capable of, my chest ached with how easily I had given into him.

I moved toward the small fire that still had deep red coals burning at its center, and I lifted my hands out, chasing their warmth.

"How did you sleep?"

I spun my head to the side at the sound of Queen Veda's voice and watched as she came up beside me. Her dark hair was pulled back at the nape of her neck, and her trousers were coated in dirt and dust from her days of travel. She held out some sort of dried meat in my direction, and I hesitated.

"I'm not going to poison you, Starblessed." She chuckled softly and held it out further in my direction. I noted the dark circles under her eyes as she raised her chin. "If I did, this would all be for nothing."

"Don't call me that." I took the meat from her hand, but I still didn't bring it to my mouth.

"Starblessed? That's what you are, isn't it?" She was studying me as she spoke, gauging my reaction to her words.

"These marks on my skin aren't a blessing." I shook my head and looked back to the fire. "They have done nothing but damn my fate."

"Your fate can't simply be damned by the way you were born." Her gaze roamed over my cheeks before falling to my shoulder. "The mark of the stars didn't curse you. It was people who did that, Adara. People who don't give a damn if they hurt you as long as they can control you and weaponize you for their own rule."

"People like you?" My mark sparked to life against my spine, and I knew Evren was near. I looked over my shoulder, and there he stood near his men and a few horses, and he nodded at something one of them was saying even though he was looking directly at me.

"I don't expect you to trust me, Adara."

I pulled my attention back to her. Her hands squeezed into fists even as her shoulders fell.

"I would question your sanity if you did so blindly, but Queen Kaida and I, we aren't the same."

My stomach hardened at her words. She was right, I didn't trust her, and I didn't think I ever would. She was the queen of the Blood kingdom, the mother of my mate, I stuttered in thought at how easily that word formed in my mind, who betrayed me, and no one becomes queen without a thirst for power.

"I apologize for not taking your word on that." I crossed my arms. "Queen Kaida would like for me to believe that she isn't nearly as bad as she truly is as well."

"That's probably true." She smiled, though it didn't reach her eyes, and gave a half shrug. "But I've never known the woman to be anything other than her true, cruel self." Her gaze dropped to my hand where I was still holding the dried meat, and she nodded toward it. "Eat. We'll be leaving for Sidra Palace shortly."

She turned, leaving me with nothing but the meat and my thoughts, and I looked back to where Evren stood. He was still watching me, his gaze hard and unreadable, but it flickered to his mother as she moved away from me.

I shoved the meat into my mouth as he took a step in my direction and quickly turned away from him. I wasn't ready to face him after last night, after I allowed him to kiss me after everything that had happened. I had kissed him with so much want laced behind my lips, and he left the tent this morning without a single word.

"You ready?"

I could feel the heat of his chest at my back, but I didn't turn around. I just stared ahead at the dying fire and nodded once. I could feel him studying me from behind, the heat of his gaze stronger than the flames in front of me, and I quickly swallowed the tough meat before wiping my mouth.

"Princess?" Just hearing his voice made my stomach tighten to the point of pain.

"I asked you not to call me that." My voice was cold and unfeeling, exactly like I wanted it, but the complete opposite of how I felt inside. The urge to make sure he was okay was overwhelming, and I was dying to know if he was plagued with his nightmares often.

"Okay." I could practically hear the frustration in his voice. "Are you ready, Adara?"

"Yes." I finally turned to him, and my eyes threatened to flutter shut as the smell of him hit me. "Your mother said we are leaving for the palace shortly."

"We are." He crossed his arms as he studied me. His black shirt was clouded with dirt, and when I looked back up at his eyes, I saw the same weariness in his gaze. "The men are going to take down our tent, and then we'll head out."

"You should have woken me." I lifted my chin as I said it. "It was foolish to let me sleep in while the rest of the camp was packed up."

It was foolish to let me sleep while you left me feeling so unsure.

I wasn't sure why that bothered me so much. He had asked me to stay with him for the night, and he didn't owe me anything this morning. But my chest ached, and I couldn't get the feeling to stop. I hated him, and the feeling confused me. How could I hate someone so badly while also craving them with every part of my being?

"You were sleeping so peacefully when I awoke. I knew you needed your rest." His gaze fell to my mouth, and I bit my tongue to stop from saying the things I truly wanted to say.

"Well, thankfully now I'm rested and thinking clearly. So we should be on our way." I went to step past him, but he stopped me with his hand on my bicep. He moved in close, close enough that everything about him overwhelmed me.

He stepped close enough that every part of me felt unsure in my resolve to hate him.

"You're angry with me."

"You're bright, prince."

His lips cocked into a smirk at my remark. "I meant angrier than normal. Angrier than you were when I left you sleeping."

My spine straightened, and I begged it not to tremble under the weight of his presence.

"I'm fine."

He leaned closer still. His nose pressed against my jaw, and I felt him breathe me in as if I was his first true breath after a lifetime of suffocation. "I'm sorry if I upset you last night."

"You didn't." My voice broke, and I hated it. "Last night shouldn't have happened. It won't happen again."

He groaned and his breath rushed out against my neck. "We both know that's a lie, princess. You can hate me in the light all you want, but the truth of us comes out in the dark. It always will."

My stomach tightened at his words, at his threat, and an ache began between my thighs. We were surrounded by a camp full of others, but it only took a few whispered words from his lips until he was all that I could see. He was everything that I could feel.

"That darkness is yours, not mine."

He chuckled soft and low, but he didn't back away a single inch. "Let some of your magic spill from your hands, princess. Let the rest of the camp see the way your magic is the twin to my own."

I clamped my hands into fists and tried to hide the dark stains that soiled the tips of my fingers, because I didn't want to see my magic. I didn't want to listen to the words he was saying.

"I've never met another living being with this magic, princess. This darkness is *ours* whether you want it or not."

I didn't know what he meant, but I didn't ask. I didn't relish in the thought of our magic having any parallel. He finally pushed away from me, and I avoided looking at him. Instead, I looked ahead to where Jorah was climbing onto his mare.

"You don't understand your magic yet, but you will. Soon enough, it will feel as vital as any other part of you."

Even as I tried to deny the truth of his words in my mind, I felt my magic course through me as if it were as crucial to me as the blood that ran through my veins.

I followed behind him as he led us to where his horse stood, and I hoped he wouldn't deny me a horse of my own.

"Where's my horse?"

"You're with me." He barely looked back at me. "We are heading into the Blood kingdom, and I want you with me."

"I'd rather walk."

Someone snickered behind me, but I didn't dare turn around to see who.

"That's not an option. You're with me."

Queen Veda was watching us, already perched atop her own horse, and I tried to force the fight down inside me.

"Adara, get on the damn horse."

My gaze hit his as his brow furrowed, and he jerked down the strap on the saddle to tighten it.

"I'll ride with Jorah." I didn't trust him either, but at least with him, I wouldn't be plagued with my warring thoughts.

"That's not going to happen." He gritted his teeth, and his hand fisted around the reins.

"I remember you telling me once that you would trust Jorah with your life. Why wouldn't you trust him with me?"

"It's not about trust, Adara. You are my mate, and you will ride with no other man than me as we arrive at my home."

I wanted to fight him more. I wanted to scream and thrash and take out every bit of anger and hurt that I was feeling at that moment. But I didn't.

Because this fight wasn't worth it. I didn't know what I was doing. I didn't have a clue what waited for me in the Blood kingdom or the fight I would face there.

I silently walked toward him and reached forward until my fingers wrapped around the pommel of the saddle, and I pulled myself up in front of him. Irritation clung to my skin as his hands met my sides and helped situate me against him.

Then I could feel it. His dark magic that called to my own. It wrapped around me, embracing me with its strength and possessiveness. Everyone else could see it too, his black magic like a thick smoke that coated my skin. It moved and enveloped me as we took off, and I tried not to allow my body to react.

But it was the only thing I could focus on as we started our journey to the Blood kingdom, and I tried to distract myself.

Evren pushed the horse hard as we galloped along the land of thick lush trees I didn't know. The horses' hooves slammed against the damp ground, and I tried to focus on the sound.

But Evren's touch and thoughts of what was to come troubled me. What would the Blood kingdom think of me? How would they react when they knew that I had been taken from the fae?

Would they welcome me, or would they be everything that I was taught to fear?

The thoughts rolled over and over through my head as we rode, and I could think of little else through the long ride.

I didn't know how long we had been riding, but my thighs had become sore and my back begged me to just lean back into Evren and give it some reprieve. But I did no such thing.

I put as much distance between us as his magic would allow and clamped my eyes closed when his power ghosted over my lips. Evren was so in control of his magic, so in control of himself, and I was falling apart on the horse in front of him.

I wondered if this was exactly what my father was trying to avoid. Would he have been so disappointed when he saw what I had become? Would he fight in ways that I hadn't? That even now I didn't have the strength to?

"Princess," Evren whispered, and my spine straightened as the sprawling city that lay ahead of us caught my attention as we topped the hill.

I tried to take a deep breath as my eyes scanned over the kingdom before me. Hills lush with wildflowers of every color led to the vast city with an array of stone homes and tall brick buildings. The sky was bright blue and the clearest I had ever seen it. It was far more beautiful than I could've imagined. Nothing like the nightmares of old legends.

"Welcome to the Blood Court."

I looked back at him, and I could see the hesitancy on his face.

"I have no interest in being welcomed to the Blood Court." My gaze dropped to his mouth, and I couldn't force myself to look away. "I am here against my will, prince."

His mouth curved up in a smirk that I hated but also loved, but it did nothing to hide the frustration that lay there. "This is my home, Adara." He nodded toward the bustling city as we moved closer. "This could be your home too."

I clamped my mouth closed as I searched the city ahead of us. I was about to enter a kingdom full of vampyres, a kingdom that I had been taught to fear my entire life, but I couldn't muster up the terror I had once felt.

Even as our horses' hooves sounded against the cobblestone streets, I felt more curious than fearful, and I hated that it was because Evren rode at my back.

I had no business feeling comfortable in his presence or beneath his touch, but I couldn't explain it. His magic was protecting me as it surrounded me, and I still felt safe in that protection.

The city was alive with sound and vampyres bustling through the street, but when they noticed us riding through, every one of them stopped. They looked so normal, so unlike anything I had been taught to fear. Much like those in my village, some were so pale their skin almost looked translucent while others were the deepest shade of black. Each one of them looked different from the other, and I studied them as I tried to find a way that differentiated them from me.

I found it odd that the queen didn't move behind her guards or allow them to shelter her, instead, she rode at the lead, and I watched as she smiled at her patrons like she was seeing old friends.

And they looked at her the same.

But they looked at Evren differently. It wasn't a friendship or simple respect that shone in their eyes. They looked to him with admiration.

Many bowed their heads or simply nodded to him as he rode past, but everyone watched him and the way he was holding me.

Were they admiring him for what he had done? Were they impressed that he was so easily able to steal the Starblessed from her betrothed with his wicked words and the gods' blessed hands?

Could they see how easily I fell for a man who promised me nothing?

What was the most shocking to me was that not a single one of them looked at me with an ounce of contempt or hunger. I was told of the vampyres' thirst for blood. It was a fact my mother had drilled into my head over and over throughout the years. That thirst ruled them above all else, but if that was true, they all hid it incredibly well.

Because they looked like nothing more than men and women who were happy to welcome home their prince. I straightened on the horse, Evren's thighs still pressed firmly against my own, and I watched them as we passed. I realized then that it was their unnatural beauty that set them apart, and I remembered my mother telling me of that fact on one of the double blood moons. It was their beauty that would draw you in. It was their looks that would make you attracted to them in a way that you couldn't resist.

Evren seemed to move closer to me, his chest pressed against my back until there wasn't a trace of air between us, but he didn't say a word.

I wasn't sure if he could sense my warring thoughts or if I should have truly been fearful of a threat, but either way, I tried not to let his touch affect me.

We rode through the streets quickly until the palace came into view. The castle was just as large as the one in the Fae Court, but it was different. The stone exterior was weathered with age and covered in mossy patches and climbing vines that beared vibrant flowers.

There was no large wall separating the castle from its kingdom. Instead, we rode directly from the street onto the courtyard, and a young man looked up from his book for only a moment to nod in his royals' direction before he lounged back on the bench and continued to read his tale.

It was the home of their royal family, but it seemed to fit in so well with all the other homes that we passed.

The queen dismounted easily, and I tried to follow suit, but Evren's magic refused to let me go. I shot him an angry look just as his feet hit the stones beneath us, but he simply lifted his hands as if he meant to help me down.

"Don't touch me, Evren, and remove your magic."

"Let me help you, princess." He lifted his hands higher, and his magic tightened around me as if it was delaying letting me go.

"I don't need your help."

Evren sighed and dropped his hands to his sides, but his magic was slower to leave me. It slithered away from me inch by inch, and I trembled as it skated over my marks.

He opened his mouth to speak, probably to correct me on how obvious my need for him was, but he closed it as soon as the sound of a woman's voice called out.

"Thank the gods!"

The sound pulled my attention away from Evren just as the woman's body collided with his, and she wrapped her arms solidly around him.

"Evren." His name was a plea on her lips, a damn plea of desperation as she clung to him, and my marks burned in a way they never had before.

I watched her as she clung to my mate. It hit me deep in my bones. He was my mate whether I wanted to admit it or not, and I could hardly catch my breath as I stared at the woman holding him.

She wore black leather trousers that fit tightly against her curvy frame and a cream top that highlighted her dark skin that was so lovely it battled with the night sky.

A night sky that was littered with stars.

Her star mark began at her elbow and moved around her bicep until it disappeared beneath her top. *She was Starblessed.*

Her fingers dug into his shoulders, and I watched as some of the tension fell from him.

This woman—she was important to him. *She was his Starblessed.*

She pulled away from him, pushing her untamed curls out of her face as she stared up and ran her gaze over every inch of him. She was checking him, assessing him for any injuries, and my gut clenched when she reached up and ran her fingers across his cheek.

Jealousy swirled through me like a beast waiting to attack, but it became feral when I noticed the scars that were littered along her forearm. Scars where she had been fed from.

My spine went rigid as I stared at them.

It was just one more lie that had fallen from Evren's lips. He told me that he had never fed from a Starblessed before. He had told me many things that I had no business believing.

A fool. I was such a damn fool.

Evren took her hands in his and held her out in front of him. "Thalia, I would like for you to meet someone."

He turned toward me then, but I couldn't take my eyes off her. And then she finally looked at me.

I could see the surprise in her wide eyes, the bewilderment as she looked back and forth between us. Her lips parted, but no sound escaped them.

"This is my Adara. Adara, this is Thalia."

"I'm not his," I quickly corrected him as I dismounted the horse, and this made her smile.

"Aren't you?" She cocked her head to the side as she studied me. "I can smell his magic all over you."

"You're familiar with his magic?" I snapped.

Her smile turned into a full grin.

"I like her." She chuckled and looked back to Evren, but his attention was on me. Watching, assessing, seeing far more than I wanted him to.

"Thalia is one of my oldest friends in this world."

"As I can see." I tried to push down the jealousy, but it was flowing from me like blood from an open wound.

Evren stepped closer to me, but I took a small step back.

"Are you jealous of my friend, princess?"

"Of course not." I swallowed and tried to make my words sound believable even to my own ears. "I don't care what you do."

"Are you sure?" His mouth cocked into the slightest grin, and my stomach flipped.

"Why would I care?"

"Because I'm your fucking mate," he growled for only me to hear, but she heard him. Her gaze met mine, and I held it. I let her feel the truth of his words even while I was trying to deny it myself.

"I am your prisoner just as I was to your brother."

Evren jolted back as if I had slapped him. He studied me, calculating what to say, and I hated this game between us. "Thalia will be with you here in the Blood Court, and she will help you adjust to your life here. Allow me to show you to your room." His words were clipped and full of anger.

He started to turn from me, but my own anger rose. I didn't want his lover catering to me while I was here. I didn't want anyone near me. "What? Are you too busy to see to me yourself?"

His shoulders stiffened, and he drew in a short breath. "I must return to the Fae Court within the coming days, princess."

FOUR

M y vision blurred, and I couldn't see Thalia anymore. I couldn't see or think about anything other than the words that had just passed his lips. He was going back. He brought me here, away from his brother, and now he was going back.

My hands shook as Jorah walked up and wrapped Thalia in his arms. He looked as genuinely happy to see her as Evren did, but it didn't matter.

He was leaving.

"I'm going to take Adara to her room," Evren spoke to them, but he was still looking at me.

And I couldn't hide a single bit of my distress.

He reached forward, gripping my elbow in his hand, and he said something under his breath, but I couldn't make it out. My heartbeat was rushing in my ears, hammering away every bit of composure I had managed to hold on to.

He was leaving.

Evren led me up the steps to the front of the palace, and I followed behind him wordlessly as two guards opened the doors for us and let us inside. Both bowed their heads in respect to my mate, and I wondered if they knew.

Did they all know they were going to be sending their prince back into the hands of their enemies?

Did they care for him at all or did they only care about what he could do for them? He was their prince but also their spy and their traitor.

I couldn't decide if he was as much a pawn in their game as I was or if that was just what he'd have me believe. Was he the master who got off on the thought that he could fool me into believing any part of him belonged to me. My chest ached as we walked into the palace. The windows were made of mosaic glass that caused the sunlight to bounce about the room, and along the furniture made of warm, aging wood. The palace was grand, but it still somehow felt like a home. We stepped into a large great room, and the smell of smoky hearths, fresh flowers, and aged books hit me. Memories of the small home I shared with my mother flooded me.

"I'll give you a tour once you're settled." Evren ran his fingers through his hair, and I watched the way the sun shined in through the windows and brought out the blaring darkness of it.

I didn't answer him because I didn't know what to say. The same thought was choking me, and I feared nothing else would escape my lips.

He was leaving.

We walked through a long hallway, the same aged stone greeting me inside the palace, but there was so much sunlight. When I had thought of the Sidra Palace, I had imagined an eerie castle that housed blood-thirsty vampyres. It was the image my mother and those in my village had painted in my mind. It was hard to wade through all the lies. They slipped through my fingers as easily as the truth, and I couldn't recognize one from the other.

"This is your room." Evren stopped in front of a large

wooden door with an ornate golden handle, and his hesitation hammered in my chest like the ghost of what we could have been. But he didn't say another word. He simply reached forward and opened it, and I followed him inside.

The door clicked closed behind me, and I tried to hold in the gasping breath that was desperate to beg him not to leave.

"My room is directly across the hall." He crossed his arms as he moved toward the bed. It was covered in layers and layers of white fabrics and fresh flowers set on the table at its side, and it wasn't lost on me that he was the one to give me this even though he had taken me in the name of his kingdom.

It was grander than anything I had ever had. The bed called to me, and my bone-deep tiredness hit me as I stared at it.

"But you won't be there."

It wasn't a question. It was the truth, and it was clawing at my chest as I glanced back to the door.

"I will be for a few days, but then no, I won't." He looked away as he said it so nonchalantly. He said it as if him leaving me didn't feal like the biggest betrayal of all.

"Why?" I shook my head and balled my hands into fists as I looked up at him.

"Why am I leaving?"

"Why would you bring me here if you were just going to leave? Why would you bring me here at all?"

"Would you rather I had left you?" He spat the words at me, and this was what I needed. His anger I could deal with because it was easier to swallow. I was angry and scared, and it was all crashing against my chest, begging for release.

"I would rather you not lie!" I stepped toward him, and my magic snaked under my skin, uncontrollable and feral. "For the first time since you've met me, just tell me the truth."

"The truth, princess, is that I have no choice but to return to the Fae Court. I cannot allow my father or the queen to think that I am the one that took you. We cannot afford for them to think anything other than the fact that we were attacked. They will know that the Blood Court took you, but I need to influence their next plan of attack."

I shook my head, but he simply continued.

"If they find out that I am the one that took you, the fae queen will not stop until I am dead and you are laid bare before them. I have to find out what they know, what they suspect."

"And what if they know the truth?" My stomach turned and chills broke out against my skin.

"Then I will be the one to deal with those consequences, and you will be safe under the protection of my kingdom."

"No." Fear clawed at me, and I balled my hands into fists as black smoke swirled around them in a mist of my terror. "I will not allow you to go back there. You are not going to get killed over me."

A smile tipped on Evren's lips, but his normal cockiness wasn't there. Instead, it was replaced with a ghost of who he was as sadness filled his eyes.

"I don't have a choice, princess. Neither of us do. This is bigger than either of us."

His gaze snapped down to where my magic was growing. It crept closer and closer to him with every breath I took, and I couldn't stop it. It was searching for him, begging him for things I wouldn't dare speak out loud.

"Of course, we have a choice." My voice was much softer than I meant it to be. It lacked conviction, lacked the anger I protected myself with.

He reached out his fingers, meeting my magic and toying with it in a gentle caress that had my breath catching in my throat and my knees threatening to buckle.

"If I had a choice, I would never go back. If I had a choice, I wouldn't have brought you here. I would have run." He stepped closer to me, my magic wrapping around him and pulling him closer still. "I would have taken you anywhere in this world where it could have just been the two of us."

"Why didn't you?" My voice was weak and full of longing for us to be anything other than what we were. The memory of what I thought we were had become a weapon, and it pierced through me effortlessly.

"Because you would have paid the price for my selfishness. You, along with all of my people, would have suffered so that I could make sure my hands never ached to touch your skin." He reached forward and his fingers, still wrapped in my own magic, grazed against my cheek. "Everyone would have paid the price for a selfish prince who wanted nothing more than to disappear in his mate." He stopped and his dark gaze searched my face. "And there is nothing in the world I want more, princess, than to disappear in you."

I stared up at him, breathless, because even though the taste of his betrayal was fresh on my tongue, I couldn't stop the next words that passed my lips with no thoughts of the consequences. "I don't want you to go."

"I know." He nodded before pressing his forehead to my own. His hand snaked to the back of my head, and he tangled his fingers in my hair as he held me against him. "But I will come back. I will always come back for you, princess."

His words crashed into my chest, but they left nothing but a deep ache. Fear, pure and unrelenting, settled deep inside me, and refused to leave.

He was my mate, but I shouldn't have cared this much. He had used me, betrayed me, and I should have been more than willing to let him go off and get himself killed. But I wasn't. His betrayal blared in front of me, but I had learned none of the lessons it was damned to teach me.

I closed my eyes and tried like hell to pull my magic back into me. "Come," I commanded it over and over in my mind. I could feel its hesitation, its own fear of letting him go, but if I was going to survive this kingdom, I needed to hold on to my anger like the lifeline it was.

I could handle it, mold it into exactly what I needed it to be, but fear I could not. My fear would damn me, but my anger would be my savior.

I pushed against Evren's chest, forcing his body away from mine, and I blinked my eyes open with my new resolve.

Don't let him in.

Evren's gaze searched my own, and he opened his mouth but I beat him to it before he could utter a word.

"Go." I nodded to the door.

"I'm not leaving for a few days, Adara."

"Go," I said again, and this time I hoped he heard how hollow I was trying to force myself to be. "I wish to be alone."

"Princess, I know you're angry, but..."

"Go!" My power surged inside me, stopping in its tracks where I was still trying to pull it away from him. It was hovering, waiting, like it had finally recognized the command of its master.

"Don't do this, Adara." I could see the spark back in Evren's gaze, his anger returning full force with the taste of mine. "Don't push me away because you're scared."

"I'm not." I shook my head and tried to solidify my lie in my own head before I spoke it aloud. "I have spent more than enough time with the man who betrayed me, and I have nothing left to spare you. I simply wish to take a bath and sleep... or is that more than you'll allow me while in your kingdom? Should I expect you to dress me up and parade me around like your brother did before you?"

I could feel his own power surging, slipping through his fingers as his anger built. He simply stood in place and stared at me as if he were trying to figure out who I was. But he wouldn't find that answer staring back at him because I didn't know the truth myself.

I was stuck in a haze of who I once thought I was and who I was destined to be, and I couldn't find my way out. Everything I thought I knew was a lie. Every certainty that I had clung to, everything that had ever felt real. It had become smoke in my hands, and no matter how hard I gripped, it slid through my fingers.

"I will give you some time." He bowed his head gently, and I scoffed at the show of honor.

"Lift your head, prince. Unless it's easier for you to tell your lies when you're bowing on your knees."

He jerked his head up until he was looking directly at me, and a dark smirk formed on his lips.

"I will do whatever you want me to on my knees, princess. You want me to breathe all the wicked fucking truths to you against your thighs? I will. You want lies? I'll worship you with my tongue while I tell you I don't linger over your curves like a man starved. I'll lie and say that your soft little moans don't torture me at night when I try to rest. I'll whisper a lie against your skin and make sure you know that my desire for you isn't the most dangerous weapon that anyone can use against me."

I sucked in a sharp breath as I choked on his words, and his gaze snapped to where my chest rose and fell with the rapid beat of my heart.

"I'll tell you that leaving you here without me doesn't feel like someone has my heart gripped in their fist squeezing tighter and tighter until I can't remember how to breathe. So, which is it, princess? Do you want my truths or my lies? I am damned to give you whatever you want despite knowing it's bad for me."

An ache deep in my belly was making it hard to cling to anything other than the way he made me want him. My body was tired, I was tired, but still I wanted to reach out for him and beg him to give me everything he had just promised. "Please get out."

He ran his tongue over his bottom lip before he reached

forward again and pressed his thumb against my mouth. His own desire was screaming at me, begging me to challenge him, to make him give me exactly what he promised.

He pressed firmly against my lip, dragging it down as he slowly lowered his hand, and he didn't stop until his hand pressed gently against my neck. His thumb rubbed against the spot where my pulse was hammering in want and confusion, and he watched the movement wordlessly.

I started to reach for him, to beg him for anything he was willing to give, when a soft knock sounded on the door. I expected Evren to drop his hand, to skirt back from me as quickly and easily as he did in the fae kingdom, but he did neither of those things. His hand tightened slightly, and moisture rushed between my thighs as I watched his want shift into anger at whoever was interrupting us.

"We're not finished with this," he leaned in and whispered against my skin, and the promise made me want to bar the door and refuse to let anyone else in.

I let out a slow, shaky breath as my pulse pounded beneath his fingers, but Evren slowly pulled his hand away from my neck and slid his gaze over my body, a measured caress as he took in every part of me.

He let out a huff of frustration before he turned from me and moved to the door. A woman a bit older than my own mother stood there with a tray of food in one arm and what looked to be clothes in the other.

My spine straightened as she stepped inside the room. My body was still thrumming from Evren's touch, and I wasn't prepared to see anyone else. It didn't matter that her face was kind and aged with years of living, I had to treat everyone in this kingdom as a threat.

"I'm sorry, Evren." She blushed, but she didn't bow her head. "I didn't realize you were in here or I would have waited."

"It's not an issue." He looked back toward me and clenched

his jaw as he crossed his arms. "Thank you for coming. Adara would like to bathe and sleep, but I'd like for her to have a warm meal first."

"Of course." The woman looked at me with a warm smile.

"Adara, this is Mina. Mina, Adara." Evren looked back and forth between us with his shoulders stiff and his guard up.

"It's nice to meet you, Mina."

"Likewise." She smiled and started to move past Evren, but he bent before she could and pressed a soft kiss to her forehead. "I'm so glad you're finally home." She closed her eyes, and her face softened as she leaned into his touch. "At least for a little bit."

"It's nice to be home." He stood back to his full height. "I missed you."

"I know, dear boy." She nodded her head. "I missed you, too."

They spoke so fondly to one another, and I watched her carefully. This woman was part of his staff, yet she looked at him with more adoration in her eyes than his own mother had. It confused me as the contradiction between what I thought I knew and the truth in front of me collided. She moved past him and headed for the small table in the room, and I tracked her every movement.

"I'll check on you in a bit," Evren said as he stood at the door, but I simply nodded as I watched her place the tray down. I swallowed hard and tried not to allow him to see the emotion that was eating me alive as Mina moved toward me. The door closed with a soft click, and we were left alone.

"I brought you some clothes." She dropped them onto the bed before pressing her hands onto her hips and assessing me from head to toe. "But Evren's right. You should eat before you do anything else."

"Have you worked for him long?" The sight of the way they

had just embraced, the respect he had shown her, was playing over and over in my mind.

"His whole life." She smiled softly, like a mother pulling up memories of her child. "That boy has been both a thorn in my side and the light of my days for years."

She laughed and nodded to the table. "Why don't you eat?"

"You know he's leaving again?" I asked the question before I could stop myself. I was desperate to know why I was the only one affected by this news.

She winced, and her aged face turned ashen. "I do."

I nodded before taking a step away from her and toward the fragrant food that was filling the room and making my stomach ache in hunger.

"I'm not happy about it," she said softly, and I stopped and turned back to look at her. "Every decision that Evren makes is a choice he's making for someone else. That boy is selfless in a way that puts himself at harm."

Her words hit me with a weight that could only be held by the truth, but my anger made everything taste like a lie.

"It's hard to love someone like that sometimes. To constantly fear for them and pray that your love doesn't break your own heart. I guess you know a thing or two about that?" She tilted her head and watched me take in her words. She was calculating, sizing me up, but I would leave her wanting.

"I don't love him." I shook my head and glanced away from her.

"Don't you?" She moved past me and busied herself with my food. "I don't know much about you, Adara. I know that you've been blessed by the stars but cursed by Evren's father. But I also know that loving that boy, if that's what you choose to do, that would be your biggest blessing of all."

FIVE

I had locked myself in my room for two days. Mina was the only one who had been in or out, but I had told her that I wanted to be alone.

Sleep hadn't cleared my head like I hoped it would. Instead, I felt more lost than ever.

I was haunted by the sound of Evren knocking on my door, of him pleading with me to let him in, when I was screaming at myself to force him out.

I held a warm cup of tea in my hands and pulled my knees to my chest as I stared out the window with a deep ache in my chest. I had a perfect view from my window, and as I opened it, I could hear the bustle of the lively city just beyond the palace walls.

Laughter rang out and met me along with the scent of delicious spices that made my stomach pang with hunger. I watched as a few people walked by, oblivious to me sitting quietly in the window, and I was so shocked by how normal it all seemed.

I was in the Blood Court, a court known for nothing but cruelty and fear, but I saw none of those things here. Not outside of the palace walls at least. The men and women who passed reminded me of home. Of people working and living, and I longed for a place I didn't even know.

I wasn't homesick because I had never loved my home. But I was yearning for a feeling I desperately wished for. I longed for that sentiment, for that nostalgia.

But it wouldn't come.

There was a soft knock on my door, and I heard Mina humming outside, hovering like I had found her to do since I had been here. I didn't know if it was due to her own motherly instincts or if Evren had asked her to do so since I had refused to allow him the task.

She walked inside before I could tell her to do so, and she came carrying another tray of food. I had only been here for two days, but already I had eaten more than I had in forever.

"I'm starting to think you're trying to fatten me up for slaughter." I laughed before looking back out the window.

"Well, right now you wouldn't be very tasty. You're nothing more than skin and bones."

Mina set my tray on the small desk before moving to look out the window at my side. "Why don't you get out of this room and go outside? Instead of trying to imagine what it'd be like from this dusty window."

"I'm okay." I shook my head. I didn't want to leave the room because leaving these four walls meant that I had to face what was outside. I had to face the truth that Evren was leaving whether I wanted him to or not.

I had to face the fact that my bones ached with the desperation for him not to.

"Evren's been by again. He wants to see you."

"I don't want to see him." Gods, I was desperate to see him, to feel him.

"I told him as such, but I don't think I can keep him away for much longer. That boy is as stubborn as you are."

"I'm not stubborn." I pulled my gaze from the window to look at her and took a long sip of my tea.

"And my tits don't touch my belly button."

My tea spewed from my mouth, and I sputtered at her words.

She simply grinned. "We can both lie to ourselves, but that doesn't make the truth any less real."

"Fine." I wiped my tea from my chin and set my cup down on the ledge. "I am stubborn, but I still don't want to see him. I know that you love your prince, but he used me. He tricked me and used me…"

"And I'd say he'd probably do it again if given the chance."

I snapped my mouth shut as she moved back to my tray and uncovered my food.

"What he did was get you out of the Fae Court. I think you know what they would have done to you there. Did you get a look at Thalia when you arrived? You would've been worse. So much worse."

I didn't say a word because I didn't know what to say. Thoughts of Thalia had flooded my mind since Evren left my room. Jealous, cruel thoughts.

Mina's words confused me. Of course, she was right about Evren getting me out of Gavril's hands, but what she said about Thalia? I couldn't wrap my head around it.

"What do you mean about Thalia? What happened to her?"

Mina wiped her hands down her apron. "You should ask Evren or Thalia about that." She glanced toward the doorway, and I hated that there was something she wasn't telling me. But her loyalty didn't lie with me.

"Do you care to run me a bath?" I crossed my arms over my chest and looked back out the window. "I'd like to clear my head."

"Of course." Mina nodded and pressed her hand to her mouth as her gaze bored into me.

She turned and walked away, and I could sense her magic

just as the water began to run in the bath chamber. I looked down at the stewed meat and bread she had brought in, and I sat down before it and forced myself to eat.

The food was as delicious as it had been since I arrived, and I stuffed bite after bite in my mouth as the words Mina had said rolled through my mind.

The smell of whatever oils Mina dropped into the bath coated my room, and I relaxed almost instantly.

Evren had brought me here. He had tricked me into thinking we were something that we aren't, but I couldn't deny the fact that for the first time in a long time, I felt safer than I had in years.

I was supposed to be in a place that I had been taught to fear my entire life, yet I felt safe.

"It's ready for you." Mina wiped her hands on her long cream skirts before pushing her hair out of her face.

"Thank you, and thank you for lunch." I nodded down to my empty plate. "It was delicious."

"You're welcome, child. Now I have other things to tend to, so get in that bath and clear your head."

I smiled despite her gruff, demanding tone. I liked Mina. A lot. She was everything I had wished my own mother to be— kind and caring.

She was so many things that my mother wasn't.

"Yes, ma'am." I shoved the last bite of bread I still held into my mouth as I passed her, and she pulled the door closed behind me.

I tugged the shirt over my head before slowly lowering my trousers, and I stared at myself in the long, gilded mirror that sat in the corner of the room. Steam was clinging to its surface, but I could still see the scars that littered my body.

Rage consumed me as I was flooded with the memories of who had given them to me. Their venom, malice, and thirst for power were scarred along my body so carelessly.

Scars that were now marked with Evren's magic. He had branded me, more than just physically, and I ran my fingers over my thigh as I remembered what it had felt like to have him cover their marks on my skin with his own.

My body responded to my own touch, but nothing like the memory of him could evoke. Every time he touched me, I became engulfed with everything that he was. He made me overwhelmed. He had me clinging to desperation.

He reduced me to a woman who would beg him for anything he was willing to give me.

I pressed my fingers into my scar, his black magic and my own starlight mixing against my skin, and I took in a shuddering breath as I slammed my eyes shut. His touch had been firm where mine was soft, his hands always so sure and skilled.

I imagined that my own were his. I envisioned the things he would say, the words he would whisper while I fell apart under his touch.

Evren didn't need to lift a finger to cause my demise. It was his wicked tongue that would do me in.

I was haunted by the things he had said before he left my room only a couple days before, words that had tortured me ever since. I forced my eyes open, staring at myself and the way my hand was slowly snaking up my thighs.

I tried to imagine what Evren saw when he looked at me. If he were here now, what would he do? What would he demand of me?

My heart hammered in my chest, and I pressed my hand at the apex of my thighs as an ache began deep within me.

I stared into my eyes for a long moment, the two colors as at war with one another as the thoughts that were racing through my mind. I moved away from the mirror and pressed my fingers against the side of the large tub. The copper was warm from the water that waited inside, and I slowly dipped my toes in before sinking under fully.

The heat of the water caressed my skin, teasing me with memories of my mate doing the same, and I pressed my head back against the edge of the tub. I tried to think of anything. Of my mother, what Queen Kaida would do, of what my future held, but every thought slipped back to him effortlessly

So, I sank deeper into the water, and I allowed myself to think of nothing else.

Shame filled me as my fingers skated over my skin and down my stomach. I clamped my eyes closed and let myself to imagine that the magic-stained fingers that now touched me were his instead of my own.

My fingers trembled as I pushed them lower and slid two fingers through my sex. As soon as I touched my small aching nub, my stomach clenched in pleasure and a whimper passed through my lips.

Evren would have swallowed the sound with his mouth. He would have demanded that I give him more, that I begged him for what I wanted, and I knew that I would have given it to him.

If he was before me now, I would have given him anything he wanted to make him destroy this ache that constantly lived inside of me when I thought of him.

I slowly rolled my fingers over my nub, and I could feel the rise of pleasure building inside of me. I was so on edge that it didn't take long. A few strokes of my fingers and constant thoughts of Evren were all I needed, and I found myself gripping the edge of the tub with my other hand as I pressed my head back and bit down on my bottom lip.

I thought of him and nothing else, and for a moment, it was as if I could feel his magic floating against my skin, caressing me and coaxing my pleasure from my body. I focused on that feeling and chased it with my own fingers against my sex, and I couldn't stop myself as I cried out his name.

My pleasure had become his and his alone, and my body knew it even when he wasn't there to command it.

My release hit me, and I clamped my legs down around my hand as it became too much.

I opened my eyes and gasped at the black magic that filled the room. *My magic.* I hadn't even realized that I had allowed it to come to surface let alone slip through my fingers that were far too busy chasing thoughts of my mate to notice my own power.

My fingers trembled as I watched the magic move around me, and I took a deep breath and sank beneath the water. I counted slowly, but it didn't matter how long I managed to stay beneath the surface. Shame ran through me, chasing away the aftershocks of my pleasure.

SIX

I wrapped the thick towel around my body and did my best to wring out my hair. My body was exhausted, my mind as well, and I wanted nothing more than to climb into my bed and sleep away the rest of the afternoon.

I wanted to sleep away the plague of thoughts about what I had just done.

I pulled the washroom door open, steam escaping with me, and I stopped short when Evren lifted his head to look at me.

He was sitting on my bed with his elbows resting on his knees and his head in his hands. He had dark circles under his eyes, his exhaustion making itself known, but I tried to not let my worry for him fester inside of me. I reminded myself of who he was, of what he was, and of the consequences his role had played in my life. It was the only way to protect myself, to protect my heart. I held on to my anger and fear as I imagined him sitting here in my room while I was on the other side of that door using my own fingers while thinking of him, of this man I should have feared above all else.

Oh gods. Had he heard me?

"What are you doing in here?" I looked back to the door, but it was fully shut, sealing the two of us off from everyone else.

"What would you have me do?" He ran his hands through his hair before letting them fall between his thighs.

"What?" I tightened my hold on my towel.

"You won't leave this room. Mina says that you refuse to let anyone in. Gods know you don't want me in here." He glared up at me in frustration. "What. Would. You. Have. Me. Do?" Every word was a clear demand for answers.

"Let me go."

"You are no prisoner here, princess, but I refuse to allow them to have you again. I cannot bear to watch my brother take from you against your will."

"Like you?" I snapped.

"You begged me."

"That was when I thought—"

"Thought what, princess?" he interrupted me before I could even form my thoughts. "That we were mates? You may hate me right now, but that doesn't change the fact that you are my mate."

"And Thalia?" My jealousy bled out even though I tried to force it down. "What about her?"

"What about Thalia?" He asked the question through clenched teeth.

"Is she simply your lover, or do you drink from her to take her power? You told me that you had never fed from another Starblessed before, but I guess everything between us was a lie."

He was a prince split between two kingdoms. Of course, he lied.

A dark shadow passed over his face, and I could see the error of my words staring back at me. "Thalia has been with me since Gavril decided he was through with her. He took every bit of power he thought he could get from her, then he washed his hands. I brought her here without his knowledge."

His words, that truth, it knocked the breath from my lungs. "She was his Starblessed?"

"She was his toy while he waited for you to come of age."

Guilt slashed through me and ate at my gut. This woman, Thalia, she had been used in ways that I couldn't even begin to imagine. Gavril had taken from me once, but the scars on Thalia's arms…

"You saved her?"

"Thalia saved herself. She fought Gavril every step of the way, and I was just her way out." He spoke in a low voice as his jaw clenched. "You could learn a lot from her. She has mastered the power that runs through her so she will never allow another to use her weakness against her again. I think Thalia could help you a lot while I'm away."

I stared at him as I considered his words. Was that really what he wanted for me? For me to become unusable in a way that even he couldn't force my hand? For me to become a weapon only I could wield?

"Thalia is one of my dearest friends. I would like for the two of you to become the same. Train with her."

"No." I shook my head. It didn't matter what he said. It didn't matter that he pointed out the similarities between us. She was a part of this court, and that meant I couldn't trust her.

"Then marry me."

I jolted back so harshly that I almost dropped my towel. Evren eyes tracked my movements with the precision of a hunter.

"What?" I shook my head as I tried to clear it. "I will never marry you, Evren."

Thoughts of what might have been flooded me, but he wasn't the man I once thought him to be. He was the blood prince, the sole heir to this kingdom that I still feared.

He grinned, but it didn't meet his hollow eyes. "I'm not asking for you to love me, princess. I don't even need you to accept that we are mates. But our marriage will protect our world."

I didn't believe a word that passed his lips. It was another manipulation, another play in his game.

"How? How is me marrying you anything more than your revenge?"

"A prince born of blood," he began, and my gaze snapped to meet his.

"Another of power. One will defeat. One will cower. The rage of the stars burned in her skin. Without her fate his rule can't begin."

I stared at him wordlessly as I played those words echoed in my head. But I couldn't make sense of them.

"That prophecy has been burned in my brain since I was a child. If Gavril is to marry you, the cruelty of my father's rule will look like child's play."

Fear like I had never known before crept up my spine and took root. "And what if the prophecy is referring to you? What if you are the one I should be wary of?"

"We both know that it isn't."

"I don't know anything." I spat as I watched him carefully. "Other than the fact that I can't trust either of you."

"How do we know the prophecy is about me? There are dozens of other Starblessed in this world. Thalia is in this palace right now." I pointed toward the door. "Marry her."

My chest tightened as I said the words. I didn't want to be used as a pawn in their game. A game among kingdoms was dangerous, and I was simply being dangled between the two princes who were both as lethal as they were powerful.

"It's you, princess." He stared up at me, and the marks on my skin came to life with his conviction. "You are the reason my father and Queen Kaida have tried to keep the prophecy hidden. I knew it the moment I met you that it was you who the prophecy spoke of. It is you who will change our world."

"I don't want to change your world." I shook my head and my wet hair slid over my shoulders. Evren tracked the movement before standing and running his hands along the front of his trousers. I didn't know what I wanted, but it wasn't this. Thoughts of Evren and I running away, of us being alone with no politics of this world to determine our future, flooded my mind. But that was a fool's dream.

I was nothing more than a girl with marred skin, and he was born to rule.

"We don't get to choose our destiny, Adara, but we do get to decide what role we'll play in it. You are inevitably linked to my family, and you have the choice between him and me. You can take my hand willingly, or my brother will force yours." His words were scathing, and his jaw clenched as he watched me.

"I don't want to choose either." Both choices invoked a fear I couldn't ignore.

His dark gaze narrowed, and I looked away from him as I said the next words. "I just want to leave."

"That's impossible." His voice lowered to a whisper as he stepped closer to me until he was standing but a breath away. He lifted his fingers, and I tensed as his skin pressed against my collarbone. He dipped his middle finger, tracing over a drop of water that had fallen from my hair, and he ran it along the length of my shoulder.

"You may hate being here with me, Adara, but letting you go would mean to allow you back into his arms. If you leave, Gavril will find you. If you choose him, I will have no choice but to respect that, but I will fight like hell to make sure you don't."

"The entire time." I stared down at his finger as it slid down my arm. "You were planning this the entire time?"

"I had no choice, princess." His hand stilled and gripped the back of my elbow. "I've seen what my brother is capable of." His hand shuddered against my skin. "But if you think for one fucking second that I regret the choices I made that got you here, you're wrong. I would do it all over again to have you standing in front of me."

"You would betray me again so willingly?"

"I would tear apart the world, princess. Even if that meant hurting you to make sure you weren't with him. I would make you hate me all over again just to make sure you were safe."

"To make sure you were here with me." His fingers trailed across my skin, tracing every inch of me with meticulous precision. "To make sure that I can touch you again."

"That's not what I want." My voice shook because what I had just said was both the truth and a lie. I wanted him, but I feared him just the same.

"Isn't it?" He leaned closer until his mouth rested against my ear. I trembled against him as I waited for him to speak again. "Your body is practically begging me for it. All I need is your words, princess."

I shook my head as moisture pooled between my thighs. Gods, I needed what he was promising. I wanted it, but I knew that I shouldn't.

A chill ran up my spine as I felt his power release from him, and before I could blink, his dark magic swirled around me.

"Just whisper it in the dark, Adara." His words echoed against my skin and his lips followed them in a gentle graze. "You are my mate, but I can be your secret sin if that's what you want. I will be whatever it takes to be able to touch you again."

His magic danced along my neck before it skimmed over my lips and stole a rush of breath from my lungs.

"I…" I hesitated and my fingers dug into my towel, the only piece of fabric separating him and me. "Please."

"You have to do better than that." His teeth grazed against my neck with a bite of pain and a soft whimper fell from my lips. "Tell me you want me. Tell me you've been dying for my touch just as badly as I have been dying for yours."

"I… want you." My voice shook just as his darkness fell over my eyes. I could still see him standing in front of me, but it was as if his magic knew. The touch of his magic against my skin, the reminder of the darkness that lay inside both of us, it was exactly what I needed. Because as much as I was dying for him, I didn't want to feel that way. I didn't want to allow myself to crave someone who was so bad for me. "Please, Evren. I want you."

The words had barely passed my lips when his hands wrapped around the backs of my thighs and lifted me against him. I didn't hesitate to wrap my legs around him as he pushed forward, and our bodies hit the wall behind me.

My words had possessed him. My own want was driving his.

His mouth came down against mine, rough and claiming, and I didn't stop him. I kissed him back just as harshly, and I hated how desperately I clung to him.

His hands were hard and frantic as they touched every part of my skin they could reach. He pressed his hips against mine, and I could feel the dagger at his side that dug into my flesh. It was a reminder that he was always ready for any threat that lay before us. It was a reminder that hit me in the chest that he was going to leave.

I whimpered against his lips, and he groaned before pushing off the wall and heading toward the doorway.

"What are you doing?" I panicked and tried to cling to the fabric of my towel to wrap it around me, but Evren's arms had me completely caged in as he reached for the handle and stormed through the door.

"Not here." He looked down at me before making his way across the hall. I didn't see anyone, but that didn't make me feel better. I was in the middle of the hall of the Sidra Palace, wrapped in nothing but a towel and their prince. "I want you in my bed."

His power shot out of him, and his door opened before we made the final step in its direction. His dark, power-laced hand lifted, pressed against my jaw, and he turned my head until I had no choice but to look back at him.

His mouth met mine again, crushing, pleading, begging, and I wanted to give him everything he asked for. In that moment, I couldn't remember why I wasn't supposed to want this man. Why I didn't want to accept his offer.

It was just me and him and my power coursing through my body and imploring me to ask him for more.

I couldn't think of what was to come. These stolen moments were all we had, and my fingers dug into his skin as I held on to it with everything I had.

Evren kicked the door shut behind him, but he didn't give me time to take in his room. He pushed across the space before he dropped me down against his bed, and I gripped his dark green bedding in my hands as I stared up at him.

My towel lay beneath me, leaving me completely exposed to him, and he rubbed his hand along his jaw as he stared. Lust and admiration. It was all I could see in his eyes, and it messed with my head.

"You are so fucking beautiful." He pulled his shirt from his waistband before reaching behind his shoulders and pulling it over his head. "I am so undeserving."

He tossed his shirt to the ground before he fell to his knees before me. I didn't have time to question if that was what I wanted. Evren quickly wrapped his hands around my thighs and jerked me to the edge of the bed before spreading me open in front of him.

"Let me show you, princess." He pressed a soft kiss on the inside of my right knee, and I jerked beneath his touch. I was wet, so wet, and I knew he could see how badly I wanted him. "Let me show you the depth of my need. How desperate I am to worship you and erase every trace of my betrayal."

I slammed my eyes closed against his words. That was everything I wanted. I wanted him to take it away, to destroy this ache inside of me, but I also knew that I needed to cling to it. I needed to remember that this man who could bring me so much pleasure was also responsible for causing so much pain. And he was capable of causing far more. If I allowed myself to forget, I feared I would lose myself completely. The future I wanted and the future destiny laid before us were vastly different. I couldn't allow myself to get lost in the fantasy and forget the truth of my fate.

His mouth moved to the other knee, his lips barely a whisper against my skin, and I tried to close my thighs as a shock wave of lust coursed through my core.

"No, princess." Evren shook his head against my thigh, and I opened my eyes to look at him. "There's no fucking hiding here. In this room, there is no pretending to be who we aren't. I am your mate, and I'm going to devour you. Now, spread your legs like a good girl and let me have what's mine."

I shouldn't have been turned on by his words. I shouldn't have loosened my muscles and allowed my outer thighs to press against the bed, but I did. I did both as I watched him lower his head and press a gentle kiss to the top of my sex.

"Eyes on me, Adara. I want to watch you as you come against my mouth."

It was impossible not to obey him, not as he breathed me in deeply, or as he licked his lips as he ran a dark, magic-stained finger down the slit of me. It was torturous watching him, and I had to bite down on my tongue to keep myself from begging.

This man was equal parts fae and vampyre, equal parts of both kingdoms I hated, and still I was willing to beg.

Evren pulled away and lifted my right thigh in his hand, kissing the inside of it before he placed it over his shoulder. "I could do this all day." His fingers dug into my flesh as he nuzzled against my leg and his breath rushed out against my sex.

"Torturing me?" I asked with a rushed and desperate voice.

"Devoting myself to your pleasure." He leaned forward and

rolled his tongue through my sex before he sucked my nub into his wicked mouth.

I cried out as my back bowed off the bed. This man had barely touched me, and already, I felt like I was falling apart.

He devoured me then, no longer giving me teasing touches or whispers of promises. He was a man starved, and he took every bit of his hunger out on my flesh.

"Evren," I cried out his name. "Oh gods, please."

His arms slid beneath me, lifting my hips off the bed, and I didn't have time to realize what was happening until he flipped us over and I was sitting on his chest. I pressed my hands into his shoulders, still desperate with want and off-kilter from the change.

"Sit on my face, princess. I want to watch you fuck your pleasure from my mouth."

When I hesitated, he took the indecision from me. His hands tugged my thighs forward, and he didn't stop until he groaned with his mouth pressed against my sex.

I ran my trembling fingers through his dark hair as I stared down at him. How could this man make me feel so wrecked with equal parts of pleasure and pain. He was everything I wanted and everything I knew I should run from simultaneously.

"Gods, you taste so fucking sweet." He sucked my nub into his mouth, and I slammed my hand against his headboard to keep myself from falling.

Everything about this was too much, yet I was desperate for more.

He was staring up at me, and I couldn't look away even though I would save myself so much heartbreak if I did. My magic was raging inside of me, begging me for release, and I wasn't sure how much more I could handle.

"Ride me, princess." Evren gripped my bottom in his hands and started moving my hips until I was grinding against his mouth. Insecurity and wavering thoughts shot through my mind before he destroyed them. "Just like that. Show me how bad you want me."

His hands stopped their movement but dug into my flesh, and I rode him just like he had instructed me to. One hand still gripping his hair, the other using the headboard as leverage, I ground down against his mouth as he sucked, licked, and nipped at my flesh.

"Oh gods." I closed my eyes as I moved harder against him. I was close. So damn close. I could feel my release rising inside me like a tsunami desperate to crash. I just needed a little more.

"Say you're my mate, Adara." My eyes flew open and slammed back into his. "Just whisper those fucking words, and I'll give you anything you want."

I shook my head as my hand tightened into his hair. It didn't matter that I knew the truth of them inside myself. Saying them out loud to him was something different entirely. I would be giving him a power I didn't want him to have.

A power I feared he would use against me. I couldn't allow him to become my weakness when my future would be determined by my strength.

A river was rushing through me, pulling me with the current, but I only wanted to stay here with him. I clung to him in desperation, because I knew the moment I opened my mouth, I would drown.

He would fill my lungs, suffocate me, and I would have no control.

I could either drown in him or get lost as I drifted endlessly.

But even that fear couldn't stop me from giving him what he wanted, from giving him the truth.

"You're my mate." The words fell from my lips, and Evren growled against me before he sucked my nub into his mouth again. His hands gripped harshly against my bottom, not allowing an inch of space between me and his mouth, and he didn't let up until my body shook against him and my screams of pleasure echoed through the room.

Pleasure was still racking through my body as I watched my magic swirling around my fingertips. Uncontrollable. That was exactly how I felt as Evren slid from beneath me and cursed as he settled behind me and ran his fingers down my spine.

I was utterly out of control.

A shock wave of want soared through me, and I gripped both hands on the headboard as I tried to put even an inch of space between us.

I could hear him working his trousers behind me, and I jerked forward again when his rough fingers pressed against my sex. He gathered the moisture there, rubbing it back and forth until I was coated from my nub all the way to my bottom.

"This is for me, mate." He growled and his voice was almost unrecognizable. I looked back at him over my shoulder as I watched him take me in. "You are fucking dripping for me." He lifted his hand and brought his dark fingers to his mouth. He looked me directly in the eyes as he slowly slid them between his lips and devoured my want from his skin as if he had never wanted to taste anything more.

His other hand was gripping his cock, rubbing back and forth as he stared at me. "Hold on to that headboard tightly." He moved closer to me and ran his length through my sex. "I have no control when it comes to you."

My fingers dug into the dark wood just as he lined himself up and pushed inside of me. My breath rushed out of me and my magic surged.

"Gods, I love seeing you like this." He pulled out of me slowly and then pushed back in, over and over, as he groaned. "That's it. You're taking me so well."

My sex clamped down around him as wave after wave of want and pleasure shot through me.

He slowly ran his hand up my spine as he thrust into me, and

I could feel my magic wrapping around his hand and arm without me doing a thing. It was as desperate for him as I was.

His hand didn't stop until he pressed it against the front of my throat, and he squeezed until I was forced to pull my hands away from the headboard and press my back against his chest.

I felt so much fuller like this, to the point I wasn't sure I couldn't handle much more.

His thumb lifted and pressed against my jaw, and he turned my head until his mouth could meet mine. He nipped at my lips before kissing me slowly and desperately while he continued to thrust into me.

His other hand slid across my breast, rolling my nipple between his fingers, and I cried into his mouth as I pushed my chest harder into his hand.

"So perfect," he murmured against my lips before dragging his hand slowly down my stomach until it met the spot where we were connected. He slid his fingers through me, but he never stopped thrusting. I didn't know what to concentrate on. I couldn't decipher which feeling was the one I was desperate to chase.

"I'm filling you up so perfectly, princess." His fingers skated over my nub, and I bit down on his bottom lip as my body shook. "You need me? You need me to fuck you until you're unable to move without remembering me inside of you?"

"Yes," I cried out and wrapped my arm around the back of his neck. He was surrounding me, filling me so fully, yet I still needed more.

I wanted to feel him like fire in my bones, burning me alive with everything that he was.

"Good girl," he whispered against my mouth just as his hand pulled away from my sex and came back down hard. The slap against my sex ricocheted through my body, and I couldn't hold it back any longer.

I cried out his name like a prayer of desperation, and he held me to him as he slammed into me over and over again. My pleasure coursed through me on the edge of pain, but it was the kind of pain I would chase for the rest of my life. He plunged inside me one final time with his hands gripping into my flesh and his low growl echoed through the room.

We sat like that for a long time. Our thighs pressed together, his arms still holding me, and our breathing ragged and reckless.

As my pleasure settled, my heart rate skyrocketed. Everything about him scared me, and I had been willing to give him too much. I gave him more than I ever should have ever allowed.

In that moment, I felt like I would follow him to the end of our world, and I would willingly destroy it to stay at his side.

And nothing frightened me more. That truth coursed through me, my magic feeling its truth with every spark of its power, and my chest ached. I had been prepared to do anything for him, all while he was lying to me.

"I need to go back to my room." I tried to pull away from him, but his arms tightened against me and his forehead pressed against the back of my neck.

"Please don't do this."

Panic clawed at my chest, a caged animal looking to rage, and I knew I needed to leave.

"Let me go, Evren. I want to go back to my room."

His hands shook against my skin, but he finally let out a harsh breath against me before letting them fall to my sides. I scrambled away from him, and I could feel the proof of what we had just done dripping down the inside of my thighs.

I quickly grabbed his shirt from where it lay discarded on the floor, and I pulled it over my head. I needed the protection, anything to put space between us.

Evren was still kneeling on the bed before me, and I could hardly look at him without feeling regret. It wasn't what we had just did that filled me with anguish. It was regrets over why we were here. Regrets over what fate had forced us into. I regretted forcing myself to take another heavy step away when every part of me was begging me to return to him.

"Stay." He reached out for me, but I took another hurried step back.

"No." I shook my head and wrapped my arms around myself as doubt and fear ate at me. "I shouldn't have let you bring me in here in the first place."

He swallowed hard as he flinched back from my words. "Don't fool yourself into thinking you didn't want this." He ran his hands through his hair, but I couldn't stop myself from looking down his body. Every part of him was chiseled from years of work and dedication. He was a warrior in every sense of the word, and it was masterful to see.

And it was just the reminder I needed to remember who he was. He was a prince first and a warrior second, and he wasn't mine at all.

"I need to leave." I looked back up at his face, and he looked so dark and beautiful still kneeling before me. "This can't happen again."

"We both know that's a lie." He climbed from the bed, and I stepped back to put more space between us. "We both know neither one of us is capable of staying away from the other."

"I don't know that." I tried to convince him along with myself.

"You are so fucking good at so many things, princess, but lying isn't one of them." He ran his thumb over his bottom lip, and I felt desperate to go to him and pull that lip into my mouth. "Your body was craving me just as badly as I was craving you."

"I'll find someone else to crave."

He stopped on his path toward me, and I could see his magic swirling in his eyes. Dirty, dark, beautiful magic.

"Don't say things like that to me, Adara." His hands fisted at his sides. "I will destroy anyone who even thinks about touching what's mine."

"I'm not yours."

"The fuck you aren't," he growled. "I'll let you keep telling yourself that if that's what you need, but just remember what you cried out to me just moments ago. Remember that I am your fucking mate, and there is no one else who can give you the things that I can."

I watched him without saying a word. My chest rose and fell harshly, and the warring feelings inside me felt like they were soon to crash.

"I hate you."

"Yet the way you fuck me says otherwise." He lifted his hand and ran the tip of his finger along his tongue. "There's a fine line between hate and love, princess, and the taste of your pleasure on my fingers tells me you loved every fucking second of what just happened."

My stomach clenched, and I reached for the door handle at my back. If I didn't leave this room, he would have me on my knees begging him for more.

It opened with a loud groan, and Evren's gaze shot to my hand. "Run back to your room." He ran his hand down his cock, and I couldn't stop myself from watching him. "I know where to find you."

SEVEN

I hadn't left my room since I ran out of Evren's several hours ago. Nor had I heard a sound from him.

I told myself it was a good thing. I couldn't clear my head. I couldn't form a single logical thought when he was around. It was like his magic, everything that he was, distorted my reality, and it was hard to remember why he wasn't good for me. The memory of his betrayal slipped through my fingers effortlessly.

But when I was alone, that was all I could think about. The way his skin felt against mine, the way my heart felt like it was crushing inside of me when I found out who he really was. Those thoughts warred inside of me endlessly, my want and my hate.

They were driving me mad, and I could handle it no longer.

The palace was quiet as I creaked open my door and peeked outside. Evren's door was securely shut, and nightfall had darkened the hallway. But even as fear tightened in my chest, my stomach rumbled. I had turned Mina away at dinner time simply because I wasn't ready to face her and know that she could possibly see the marks of him along my skin.

I was barely able to look at myself in the mirror.

I gently shut the door behind me before slipping down the hall in search of the kitchens.

I passed by doorway after doorway of rooms I didn't know, and I realized that I had seen very little of this palace. Almost every moment I had spent here, I had been locked inside my room. But the kitchen was typically the heart of the home, and I assumed that meant no different to the royal family.

I headed back toward the main entrance where I spotted two of Evren's guards standing near the door. Neither noticed me, so I pressed my back against the wall and slowly slid to the left until I was completely out of their view.

The last thing I needed was for one of them to alert Evren that I was out here. I didn't need him finding me in the hall, especially when I was still sore between my thighs with memories of him.

I looked back around the corner as my chest tightened. My stomach was in knots with thoughts of Evren and the way I had let him rule over my body so easily, but the farther I moved through the castle, the more unsettled I became. This was more than the regret I knew I should have felt. Something wasn't right.

I couldn't explain it, but something in my gut churned with dread. It had pulled me from my sleep, and at first, I thought it was simply the uncertainty of everything, but the farther I got from my room, the more panic pulled at me.

My magic prowled inside of me. I could feel it as if it were as worried as I was, and my chest rose and fell harshly with each of my breaths.

Something was off.

I just didn't know what that something was.

I let my hand drag along the rough stone of the walls as I continued to walk under the oil lamps and the smell of bread had me stopping near a heavy set of double doors.

The doors were wooden and intricately carved, and I pressed my trembling hand against one as I hurriedly pushed inside.

The kitchens were dark, save the lit candle by the oven, and I cursed under my breath for not bringing one with me. There was no way I was going to be able to find anything in here without some light.

I pushed across the room to grab the candlestick from where it sat, and I jumped when the sound of someone clearing their throat caught me off guard.

"Shit, sorry." The male laughed as my back slammed into the counter behind me. "I didn't mean to scare you."

"Who are you?" I took another step away from him, and he grinned. He was sitting on top of the counter across from me, and he had a plethora of meats, cheeses, and breads laying at his side.

"I should probably be the one asking you that since you're the stranger in our castle." He cocked his head to the side, and his long hair slid over his shoulder. He tucked his brown hair behind his ear before taking a bite of cheese as if he was completely unbothered by seeing me here.

"I'm not a stranger. I'm a prisoner." I took a few more steps away until I was able to reach the candle. Hot wax dripped down on my hand, and I winced but didn't dare drop it.

I moved it closer to the stranger in front of me so I could see him better. My heart was hammering in my chest, and I couldn't stop that deep gnawing in my stomach.

"A prisoner?" He laughed and lounged back on his hands. "Our prisoners don't have the privilege of sneaking around the kitchen for a snack in the middle of the night."

"But you do have a lot? Of prisoners, that is."

"We have a few." He watched me, and I could practically feel him calculating my every move.

I attempted to do the same to him. He was dressed in all black, so similar to Evren, but his shirt was only buttoned about halfway up his chest as if he couldn't be bothered to finish the rest of the task. Blades were strapped along his torso, and I wondered what he needed so many blades for in the middle of the night.

"And trust me, Adara, none of them are treated as you are." Hearing my name fall from his lips put me on edge.

"So, you do know who I am."

"Of course, I do." He chuckled and ran his hand over his full lips. "Do you really think our prince could bring you back here and the entire kingdom wouldn't know of it?"

"Because of the prophecy?"

His eyes widened, but only for a moment before he smoothed out his features.

"Because of everything he's sacrificed."

"Who are you?" I held the candle higher, and a dimple marred the handsome lines of his face.

"Sorin." He held his hand out in my direction. "I am the captain of the Blood army, and one of Evren's best friends."

I narrowed my eyes at him. "So, you're the captain of the Blood army and Evren is the fake captain of the fae?"

He simply grinned harder.

"Well, I guess technically he is if we're referring to Prince Gavril's men who are meant to do nothing but prance around his castle and protect his ass. Then yes, he is their captain."

"And what is it that your men do?"

He sobered then, the smile dropping from his face. "We protect this kingdom and everyone who our prince serves."

His answer angered me, fueled a hate inside me I couldn't tame. "And those were your men who attacked us in the woods? What exactly were you trying to protect then, Captain?" I couldn't forget that the men who came for me in the forest, the ones who tried to take me from Evren, had been wearing the uniform of Sorin's army.

"Those men did not belong to me." He leaned forward and his hands gripped the edge of the counter. "Those are the queen's guard."

"And you do not serve your queen?" There was a bite to my voice, and I hoped that he could hear it.

"I serve anyone my prince tells me to, but that attack to get you here before Evren was ready was not my doing."

"I don't trust any of you." I shook my head and tightened my grip on the candle.

"That's smart. You shouldn't trust anyone but the prince."

"I trust him least of all."

That smile cursed his lips once more, deeper and truer than the one before it. "Are you hungry, Adara?" He motioned toward the food at his side, and my stomach groaned. "I know you didn't just come to the kitchens because you heard that's where the roguishly handsome captain hangs out."

I set the candle down on the counter near him before hoisting myself up and sitting on the other side of the food. I picked up a piece of bread, and it smelled divine.

"It's weird." I cocked my head and looked over at him. "No one but you has described you that way."

He let out a choke of a laugh, and I didn't dare tell him that I hadn't talked to anyone about him at all. I knew nothing about this male except for the fact that he was as handsome as he was arrogant.

"If it was Mina, that's not fair. She's still holding a grudge for that time I accidentally set Evren's room on fire."

"What?" My gaze slammed into his as he laughed.

"Don't look at me like that." He held up his hands in defense. "Evren had just set a pig loose in my bedroom, but everyone seemed to forget that little detail once the fire broke out."

There was an awkward silence between us, and I shifted against the counter as I tried to imagine a younger Evren.

"Are you…" I started my question without thinking but stopped myself and shoved a bite of food in my mouth.

"Am I what?" His gaze roamed over my face, and I felt self-conscious under his inspection.

I swallowed before wiping my hand over my mouth. "Are you a full-blooded vampyre?"

Sorin grinned harder than before and a flash of his teeth glinted in the candlelight. "I am." He nodded. "Most of the people you will meet in this kingdom are."

"But you don't want to bite me?" My question sounded foolish even to my own ears, but I was still embarrassed when Sorin started laughing so hard that he held his hand against his stomach.

"Is that truly what you think of us? That we just go around draining the blood from every human we meet?"

I thought about everything I had ever read and learned about the vampyres of this realm, and that was exactly what I thought. It was all I had ever known until I met Evren.

Sorin must have seen the truth on my face because he continued without me answering him. "Your histories of us are incorrect. Our thirst for blood has been honed into a weapon, but we aren't walking around like crazed monsters desperate to taste you."

He lifted a piece of meat between his fingers. "Most of us drink from animals when the need arises. Some of us drink from humans who are more than willing to allow such a thing."

"What?" I jolted back in shock.

"When Evren fed from you, what was it like?" His gaze was serious, searching.

My back straightened at his question. "How do you know he's fed from me?"

"There are many ways that I know." He cocked his head and ran his tongue over his bottom lip. "But the most predominant one is because Evren told me. Close friends, remember?"

"When he fed from me it was..." I could feel my blush heating my cheeks.

"It brought you pleasure, did it not?"

"Did he tell you of all the lies he fed me to make me feel the need to let him feed from me?" I crossed my arms over my chest.

Sorin was quiet for a long moment before his gaze ran over me slowly. "It's a shame that the two of you are mates. Without that, I may have stood a chance at stealing you away from him." His tone was teasing, and I had a feeling he was trying to get a rise out of me.

"We are not mates," I growled the words between my teeth. It didn't matter that he was right. I hated that everyone knew the truth so easily when I had just come to accept it myself.

"It doesn't matter that you say those words with so much conviction, Adara. You cannot change who your mate is simply because you wish it so."

I didn't say a word. I simply stared at him as I thought about what he said.

"I can smell him, feel his magic radiating off your skin." His gaze ran over my face. "There isn't a single chance of you hiding it."

My stomach hardened, and I tried to swallow down my emotion. "Where is he?"

His gaze darkened, and I hated the feeling it gave me.

"Is he in his room?"

"He didn't tell you?" He watched me carefully, too carefully.

"Tell me what?" My heart hammered in my chest, and I pressed my fingers against my thighs to keep them from trembling. "What don't I know?"

"He left tonight under the cover of darkness. He and Jorah are headed back to his father's kingdom."

Everything stopped as I stared at him and tried to take in his words. I couldn't catch my breath, and my chest ached to the point of pain.

"He went back?"

"You say that like he has a choice." There was an edge of anger in Sorin's voice. "Our prince may be a lot of things that you think about him, but he has lived a life of sacrifice for his people."

I could hear the truth in his words as I gasped for breath. I pressed my hand against my chest in an effort to relieve the tension that pulled there. He brought me here then he left me. He left me, and he didn't dare say goodbye. My heart hammered as anger fueled me, but there was also so much regret. I should have spoken to him instead of storming out of his room. I should have told him the truth about how torn I was over the need to protect myself and the need to be near him.

"He left me."

"He will do whatever it takes to protect our people. He has spent his entire life making sure we weren't destroyed under his father and brother's rule."

Sorin slid off the counter and moved in front of me. He stared up at me as if he needed my full attention for the next words that passed his lips. "The people of this kingdom will follow Evren blindly wherever he asks them to go. We will do anything he asks of us, and we aren't willing to do that because he's like his brother. He is everything that his brother is not."

"And what if you're wrong?" I could hear the fear in my voice, the desperation to believe what he said about Evren to be true but the fear that it wasn't.

"If you believe that"—he shook his head softly as he started walking toward the door—"then you don't know your mate at all."

EIGHT

I t had been two days since Evren left. Two days of
excruciating worry and fear. Emotions that ate at me even
though I reminded myself repeatedly of who he was and what
he'd done. But I had no choice in how I felt.

It wasn't a choice, and I feared what would happen to him if
Queen Kaida already knew of his treason. It wouldn't matter that
he was the son of her king. He would become a traitor above all
else.

All because he had taken me.

A loud knock sounded at my door and had me looking away
from the window. The knock sounded again, hard, loud, impa-
tient, and my gut sank.

My heart lodged in my throat. What if it was Evren?

Could he be back so soon?

I rushed toward the door and jerked it open. I pushed my hair
out of my face, and I couldn't hide my desperation that it was
him on the other side of that door.

Even through my fear of who he was, I would have given
anything for it to be him.

But I stopped in my tracks when I came face to face with Thalia leaning against my doorframe. Clothing dangled from the crook of her arm, and she watched me in a way that was so calculating yet so unbothered. She was a Starblessed, but that didn't mean we had any similarities between us. She was a member of this Blood Court, and I was cautious of her as I was everyone else.

"Can I help you?" I straightened out the simple dress that Mina had left for me this morning, and Thalia tracked the movement, taking in my nervous tics for exactly what they were.

"Were you expecting someone else?" Her dark gaze fell upon mine, and I quickly shook my head.

"I was kind of hoping you were lunch."

"That'll have to wait." She straightened to her full height, a few inches taller than me, and tossed the clothing in my direction. I was forced to catch them, and I tugged them close to my chest as I looked up at her like she was crazy. "Get dressed."

"I am dressed." I looked down but stopped short at the sound of her scoff.

"Change out of that ridiculous dress. You can't train for shit in that. I'll wait for you in the hall."

Train. "I told Evren that I wasn't interested in training with you."

"Well." She looked back at me, and I could see something in her eyes that both scared me and fueled me at the same time. "I'm not sure if you're aware or not, but your mate isn't here." She simply shrugged her shoulders. "And I'll be damned if I allow you to just mope around in this room for any time longer. Now get dressed."

She didn't wait for my response. She simply stepped back and closed the door behind her to give me privacy.

I stood there for a long moment, staring at the door where she had just been, and I could feel my anger rising. My anger with her, with Evren, with everything.

I moved to my bed and jerked my dress over my head and kicked the useless slippers from my feet. I pulled on the black leather trousers Thalia had brought, and they fit me as if they had been made for me. I pulled my old boots from the small trunk at the end of my bed before sitting down and pulling them on.

Already, I felt better. I felt some sense of power fueling me.

I tucked my dagger into my boot before pulling the black shirt over my head and tucking it into my trousers. It was a bit loose, and the neckline fell at the top of my breasts.

But it was so much more me than the dress I had just torn off.

I stood and moved to the door even though a part of me wanted to refuse her. A much bigger part of me wanted to know about Thalia. I wanted to know what she had been through, who she was to Evren, and if it took training with her to learn these things, then I would do it.

Because deep down I knew I wouldn't survive this world if I didn't learn to control my magic. I wouldn't survive at Evren's side or if I left.

As soon as I pushed through the door, Thalia looked me over once before she started walking down the hall. She was silent as I followed her, only the sound of our footsteps and my rushed breathing meeting us.

"Where will we be training?" I pulled my hair over my shoulder as I followed her and quickly tried to twist it into a plait.

"The back courtyard," she answered without ever looking at me. "We'll have plenty of space out there."

"Okay." We passed by the open doors to the kitchens, and I nodded at one of the cooks who watched us as we went by. "And what are we going to be training exactly?"

"How to make you not weak." Thalia stopped and held the door open for me, and I narrowed my eyes.

"I'm not weak," I practically growled the words, and that drew a smile to her lips.

"Prove it." She motioned for me to go outside, and I lifted my chin as I did so.

The courtyard was a large, open space that was surrounded by flowers of every color. The flowers grew wild, far less manicured than the fae kingdom would ever allow, and I smiled at the vines that were creeping up the edges of the castle and coating it with their yellow buds.

It was breathtaking.

"Go ahead and set your weapon to the side."

I spun around and faced Thalia, who was rolling up her sleeves. She wasn't paying one bit of attention to the flowers, hers was completely focused on me.

"What weapon?"

She cocked her brow at me, but I knew she wasn't a fool. "The one hiding in your boot. You won't need it today. We'll work with daggers another day."

I hesitated as my heart rate spiked. I didn't want to drop my dagger. It was right where it belonged, and I hated the fear that hounded me at the thought of not having it at my side.

"Drop it, princess."

"Don't call me that." I crossed my arms and Thalia grinned.

"Why not? Isn't that what your mate calls you? What did Gavril call you? His precious? His love? How many pet names did you have in the fae kingdom?"

My anger rose inside me, and I could feel my power rising with it. "Gavril referred to me as the Starblessed."

"Of course, he did." She shook her head as a small, harsh laugh fell from her lips. "I would expect nothing less from the asshole."

"I take it you don't like Gavril?" I watched her carefully. I knew in my gut that what Evren told me about her was true, but part of me needed to hear it from her.

"I'll be the one to kill him." She looked at me, and I could see the truth pouring out of her. "I will allow Evren to do whatever it is he needs to do to ensure the safety of our kingdom, but once that is done, it will be my blade that ends Gavril's rule."

The anxiety coursing through me loosened at her words. She hated him as much as I did, far more than I ever could, and that made me trust this girl more than anything else could.

"Okay." I nodded and pulled my dagger from my boot with trembling fingers. I set it down carefully to the side, and she watched my every move.

"What would you like for me to call you?"

"Adara." I straightened and ran my sweating hands down the trousers she had given me.

"Okay, Adara." She bowed her head gently. "How did you learn to use that dagger?"

"Trial and error." The words slipped past my lips, and Thalia laughed. "It belonged to my father, and after I learned what the Achlys family did to him, that they killed him, I promised myself that I would learn to use it, to hold it."

I had practiced with the blade day and night when I was old enough to learn what they had done to my father, when I learned of my fate. Nightmares plagued me, memories of him I wasn't certain were real, and his dagger in my hand was the only thing that kept them at bay.

She nodded as if she understood, and I wondered what horrors this girl had been through. Had she lost family too?

"So, no official training?"

"No." I shook my head. "What I know is through my own practice and sneaking to watch some of the men in my village."

Thalia nodded before waving me forward. I met her and bent at the knees as I watched her assessing me, calculating. "The first thing you need to learn is hand-to-hand combat. Most of the men we encounter think we're nothing more than useless women. Prove them wrong."

"Okay." I nodded and missed the way her leg swung out and hit the back of my calves. It caught me completely off guard, and I fell to my ass with a loud huff.

My power grumbled in my veins, begging to be released, as my hip ached from my fall.

"Get up." Thalia motioned for me to stand. Ordered me to do so.

I wanted to refuse, to fight against her, but I knew that would do me no good. So, I shoved it down. I tried to drown my power in my anger as I stood and dusted off my trousers.

"I wasn't ready," I gritted the words through my teeth.

"Be ready for anything, Adara. These people aren't going to wait until you're in position to attack you." She rubbed her hand down the back of her neck. "We should start with the basics."

"I think I know the basics."

"I think your stance is weak." Thalia's gaze ran down my torso, and I tensed under her assessment. "We need to work on that and build strength before we do anything else."

"I thought we were going to fight." I pressed my hands to my hips and looked around us. "Evren told me you were going to train me to use my power."

Thalia bounced on the balls of her feet as she assessed my own. "If we fight right now with our powers or without, I'd end up hurting you, and I really don't want to have to explain that to my prince."

Her prince. Jealousy reared its ugly head even though I didn't want it to. "I don't have to explain anything to him."

Thalia laughed then swatted at my thighs gently. "Widen your stance a little. Find your balance."

I did as she said, and she grinned victoriously.

"So, what's the deal with you and Evren?" She moved around me and pressed her hand against my spine. She used it as a board as she wrapped her other hand around my shoulder and forced it back until I stood straight. "Are you just trying to fuck with him by denying the fact that you two are mates? No judgment." She laughed and held up her hands as she moved back in front of me.

"No." I shook my head. "I'm not fucking with him. I don't want to be his mate."

She looked up at me and the light dimmed in her eyes. "You do realize that it's not a choice, right? It's not a choice for either of you."

"I know." I quickly looked away from her. "But that doesn't mean I have to act on it. That I have to allow it."

"From what I hear, you certainly aren't *not* acting on it."

I stiffened and my gaze slammed back into hers. "And where did you hear that?"

She reached forward and her fingers tapped against my neck. "That little mark right there didn't happen by itself, unless you've found someone else in the castle."

I could feel my blush creeping up my chest and into my face as I clamped my hand down over my neck. "That was a mistake."

"No." She shook her head. "He is your mate. Do you know why everyone seems to already know that fact before you ever open your mouth to tell them?"

I opened my mouth to argue, but she was right. So many had known we were mates before either of us had ever uttered a word.

"Mates are rare these days." She gripped my hand in hers and balled it into a fist. She fixed each finger until they were perfect as she spoke. "Mating between a vampyre and a Starblessed is even rarer. I've never heard of such a pairing."

"You think we shouldn't be together?"

"What?" She pressed her hand against my elbow and lifted my arm until it was exactly where she wanted it. "That's not what I'm saying at all. The two of you have every reason not to be together, every possible force trying to tear you apart, but still, he is your mate."

"He lied to me about who he was." My hand trembled.

"And he saved you." She looked up at me and there was so much pain staring back at me. "He told me that Gavril took from you before you left."

I winced, but she still held my hand firmly in her own.

"So, I don't have to tell you how horrible it is, how horrible he is, but he is capable of so much worse." Her gaze ran over my face, and I could see her memories raging inside her. "He would have been so much worse, Adara."

"He's the one…" I looked down at her scarred arms and swallowed harshly as I thought about the sheer amount of times he had to take from her.

"Yes." She nodded and stood straighter. "Every scar that lines my body is from the crowned fae prince, and I will never allow him to take from me again. Evren helped me ensure that his brother would never be able to do so again."

Her words hit me in my gut because she was speaking truthfully. This woman had endured far more than I could ever fathom, and still she stood at Evren's side.

"And you trust Evren completely?"

"With my life." She nodded once before taking a small step back. "I would give my life to protect our prince, and as his mate, I will do the same for you." Her hand came down and patted me on the stomach, and I let out a harsh breath due to her declaration and her hand. "Now we need to work on your breathing."

"I'm breathing just fine," I gritted through my teeth.

"No. You aren't." She took a deep breath, and I watched her chest rise and fall. "If you want to be a weapon, you must be able to control the things inside you that are needed to cleave this world." She tapped against my thigh. "Your balance and your breathing are two of the most important things. Without those, nothing else matters."

"Okay." I nodded and tried to focus on what she was saying. I tried not to think about where Evren was at that moment or the danger he was putting himself in.

I forced myself not to think about why I cared.

Instead, I focused on Thalia, and I was cursing her by the end of our training session. Sweat was rolling down my back, and my legs throbbed as I made my way down the hall to my room.

"Wait up," Thalia called out before jogging in my direction. I leaned against the wall because I was certain I would fall without it.

"I can't handle any more today." I wiped my brow with my sleeve. "Call me weak all you want, but I need a long, hot bath."

Thalia snorted before shoving a book in my direction. "This is for you."

The book was bound in brown leather that was fraying on the edges, and no writing creased its bindings. "What's this?" I quickly flipped through the pages and stopped when I saw a drawing of a Starblessed.

"It has a lot of our history." She shrugged. "Evren said that you were a reader, so I wanted to give you this in case you were interested."

I pushed off the wall before I could think better of it and wrapped my arms around her. "Thank you." My power writhed inside me, and the book burned in my hand. I barely knew Thalia, but already she felt like more than just a member of the Blood Court. She felt like my ally, and this book she had just given me, this knowledge into who I was, meant more than I think she could ever realize.

"You're welcome." She pulled away quickly and pushed her hair out of her face. "Now get some rest. We'll start again early tomorrow."

"Okay." I nodded and held the book close to my chest as she

left me standing there. I forced my stiff legs to move and headed toward my room. I flipped the book open again, the scent of old paper calming my racing heart, and I smiled.

I made it to my door but hesitated as my power pulled inside me. I glanced back over my shoulder and my gut twisted as I stared at Evren's door. *He's not there.* I repeated the words over in my head and tried like hell to get my power to understand.

But it wasn't just my power that needed him, that was going insane with worry. Thalia had distracted me, but now there was no one to keep my fear from destroying me.

I pushed across the hall and ran my hand over his door. The aged wood was smooth beneath my fingers, and I found myself reaching for the handle with trembling fingers.

I should have gone back to my room, but I twisted the handle and was shocked when it opened without an ounce of resistance. I quickly stepped inside and closed the door behind me. His room was dimly lit by a small fire that Mina must have kept going for him, and his bed was still rumpled in the way he left it.

I moved toward it, careful and shaking. The scent of him was overwhelming as I sat down on the edge of the bed and allowed my fingers to clutch the linens.

I took a deep breath, breathing in the memory of him, and something deep inside of me settled. This was his room, his home, and I shouldn't have been there.

But that didn't stop me from kicking off my boots or stripping out of my sweaty clothes. I truly needed a bath, but I couldn't force myself to leave his room.

Instead, I grabbed a black shirt that was thrown haphazardly over his chair and pulled it over my head. I was instantly engulfed by the smell of him, and I lifted the neckline and pressed it against my nose.

Just a few minutes. That was all I needed. A few minutes and I would disappear from his room as if I had never been there at all.

That was what I told myself as I climbed into his bed and pulled his dark covers up over my shoulders. A few minutes alone in his bed, and the ache I felt over him being gone would start to disappear.

NINE

I covered my head with my blanket as the loud banging continued. I wasn't ready to wake up or face whoever was waiting for me on the other side of that door.

I groaned and pressed my pillow to my face as I tried to block them out. My pillow that smelled exactly like Evren.

Evren, whose room I was currently invading.

"Shit." I threw the pillow to the end of the bed as I shot up and looked around me. The sun was shining in through the window, and it gave me no chance to pretend that I hadn't spent the entire night in Evren's bed.

"Wake up, Adara!" Thalia's voice rang through the hall, and I cursed again as I jumped from the bed.

My muscles were still stiff and achy, but I didn't have time to deal with that right now. Instead, I ran to the door and pulled it open before Thalia alerted the whole damn castle that I was missing.

"I'm up."

Thalia swirled in my direction, a new set of clothing resting in her arms, and the annoyed look on her face fell as soon as she spotted me in Evren's doorway.

"What are you doing?"

"Sleeping." I crossed my arms and prayed that she didn't make a big deal of this.

"Okay." She nodded and moved across the hall to hand me the clothes. Her gaze danced with humor and a grin graced her lips. "Get dressed, then let's get some breakfast. We have training to do."

"Right." I pulled the clothes to my chest as I shut the door and took a deep breath. I hurried to Evren's bathroom and got myself ready for the day.

My hands trembled as I shoved my legs into the trousers. I was excited for our training today, excited to feel more in control of my power. But I was also flustered by the fact that she had just found me in Evren's room, that I had felt the need to be here in the first place.

Thalia had brought an outfit that looked almost identical to the one from the day before. I looked at myself in his mirror as I tucked my shirt into my trousers, and I didn't have a clue what I was doing.

I still smelled like him, my hair, my skin. The memory of him was floating along every inch of me, and I hated to admit how much comfort it brought me.

I had no plan for what I wanted, for what I would do, but it would be foolish of me to not soak in every bit of training Thalia was willing to give me. Her help was far too valuable. I pulled my hair back away from my face and tucked my dagger back into my boot.

I was just about to leave the room when I passed by his small desk and spotted something shining in the sunlight. I stopped, my hand aching to reach forward and find out what it was.

I pushed the few sheets of parchment to the side and stared down at the delicate gold chain. I lifted it in my fingers, careful not to harm it, and stared at the small crescent moon that dangled from the chain.

There was a small tag attached to it, and my name was written across it in crisp, masculine letters. There was nothing more. No indication of where it came from.

It could have been Evren's or someone else's, but I had never seen him wear it. But the metal had a familiarity to it I couldn't explain. I could feel it as the gold pressed against my fingers.

The necklace called to me, and I gripped it in my fingers as I thought about putting it back where I found it. But that churning in my gut wouldn't stop.

Before I could think better of it, I pulled off the tag and slipped the gold chain over my head and tucked the crescent moon between my breasts. The metal hummed against my skin, but I tried to ignore it as I made my way out of Evren's room and closed the door behind me.

"Took you long enough." Thalia pushed off the wall where she was leaning next to my door. "I thought I going to have to come in and rescue you, but I didn't know exactly what was going on in there." She grinned, and I let her quip roll off my back.

I started walking down the hallway toward the courtyard where we had trained the day before, and she jogged to catch up with me.

"What'd you think about the book?"

Shit. I completely forgot about the book. I was pretty sure it was still sitting somewhere in the mess of Evren's bedding.

"I didn't get to it." I ran my hand down my face and over my neck. The gold still buzzed against my skin, and I let my fingers trail down the length of it. "I fell asleep as soon as my head hit the pillow."

"You must've been really comfortable." Thalia bumped her shoulder against mine, and I could feel a blush of embarrassment creeping up my chest.

"Are you going to tell anybody about this?" I didn't know why, but the thought of Sorin or anyone else finding out about the poor little Starblessed sneaking into their prince's room in the middle of the night while he was gone didn't sit well with me.

It made me feel weaker than I already was.

"Your secrets are yours and yours alone." She looked at me sincerely, and I trusted her word. "But you might want to think about the staff. Mina was already in a tizzy over the fact that you didn't open your door for dinner last night."

"Shit. I didn't think about that."

"It's not a big deal." Thalia turned until she was facing me and walked backward toward the courtyard. "Mina's nosy, but she won't tell anyone. Just tell her you'll be sleeping in Evren's room if that's what you want."

My chest ached as I thought about what she just said, and I open my mouth to ask her a question before I could think better of it. "And what do you think about me sleeping in his room last night? That it was foolish of me?"

"I think that you're confused." She looked at me with sympathy, and I hated it. "And that your mate brought you here to a kingdom you don't know and then put himself at risk once again. It's okay for you to be angry with him, to hate him even if that's what you feel, but it's also okay for you to worry about him. To miss him. Crave him."

My steps faltered as I looked up at her. "I don't crave him."

"Like I said, your secrets are yours alone." She winked at me, and I knew that she could most definitely see my blush now.

We pushed outside into the courtyard, and before she could ask, I set my dagger down along the edge. "What are we working on today?"

"More of the same." She bounced on her toes. "We need to focus on building your balance and your strength if you're to get anywhere else, then we'll work on your magic."

I was caught off guard by her words. I hadn't thought we would get to it so quickly. "My magic?"

"Yeah." She motioned toward my hands that were still

stained black from where I had used my magic before. They resembled Evren's hands after he used his power, but I had seen no one else with the same markings, not in this kingdom or beyond it. It was only him and I. "Your magic is different than mine. I'm not quite sure how different, but it appears to resemble Evren's much closer than it does my own."

"Do all Starblessed have magic?"

"No." She shook her head. "And most don't realize the magic that's inside them until they are fed from. I didn't have a clue until Gavril took and took and took from me." Her gaze darkened as she spoke. "I could feel it stirring inside me then, but I didn't know how to control it. It wasn't until I came here, until Evren helped me train, that I realized just how much power I held."

My chest ached for this woman in front of me. For everything that she had endured and survived. When I first laid eyes on her, I had hated her, envied her for the things I thought she had done, but every bit of that had dissolved and had been replaced with something new.

"Okay." I nodded and widened my stance just like she had shown me the day before. "Tell me what you want me to do."

By the time we got through the first portion of the training, I was sweating, out of breath, and certain I would wake up with several bruises in the morning. Thalia had taken it easy on me the day before, and even that had been hard. But today? Today she showed me what she was capable of.

I lay against the ground and shielded the sun from my eyes.

"Take some deep breaths and get a drink of your water." She was barely breathing hard. "This is going to seem like nothing once we begin training with your magic."

"What?" I looked over at her and groaned as she smirked. She had her elbows resting on her knees and a cup of cold water in her hand, thanks to Mina. Mina who had said nothing to me about the night before, thankfully.

"What we just did is physically taxing." She motioned to the small ring we had created. "But magic drains you from within. It takes so much concentration and skill, and it will drain you in a way you have never experienced before."

"Way to sell it, Thalia." Both of our heads jerked up at the sound of Sorin's voice. He was sitting on a low stone ledge that wrapped around the courtyard, and neither of us had noticed his presence. "I bet the girl can't wait to get started now."

"Don't you have somewhere better to be, Sorin?" Thalia rolled her eyes at him. "Bashing someone's head or something?"

I looked back and forth between them, and I was so confused. They both claimed to be Evren's close friend, yet they looked at one another as if they were more than willing to kill the other.

"And miss this?" Sorin leaned forward, resting his elbows on his knees. His hair was pulled back at the nape of his neck, and he somehow looked more handsome than the night I met him. "I wouldn't dare."

Thalia growled low and only loud enough for me to hear, but Sorin's handsome face lit up in a smirk that told me he knew exactly what he was doing.

"Are you two friends?" I motion back and forth between them, and Sorin laughed.

"The best of friends." He grinned "Thalia just doesn't like to admit it."

"I never denied we were friends." Thalia pushed up off the ground and stood. "You can be my friend while I still think you're nothing but a brute."

Sorin assessed her, his gaze roaming over every inch of her body before he stood with a large grin on his face. He dusted off his trousers nonchalantly, but I noted the dagger that was strapped to his thigh and two larger ones that were crossed along his back. "I could show you exactly what kind of brute I could be if only you given a chance."

I blushed and quickly rolled over onto my stomach as I

pushed up on trembling, tired arms.

"Be careful of this one, Adara. He'll try to get in your pants any chance you let him."

Sorin cocked his head to the side and studied her, but his grin never slipped from his face. "You do realize that's a you and me thing, right?" He moved his hand back and forth between them. "You're the only one I've been pining after for all these years."

I stood next to Thalia, and she tried to look so stubborn, but she couldn't hide the way her lips twitched at the side or how her shoulders relaxed. She may have been annoyed by Sorin, but she was comfortable with him. I wondered if the two of them had done far more than either were willing to admit.

"Do you mind, Sorin? We have training to get back to."

"Of course." Sorin bowed playfully with his hand resting over his heart. "I just came to relay some news about our prince."

Everything stopped in that moment. I could feel my heart hammering away in my chest. He had news of Evren. News that he was waiting until now to deliver?

"What of Evren?" I clenched my hands into fists and tried to stop myself from fidgeting.

Sorin's gaze swung to meet my own before he answered. "He's made it back to the fae kingdom. From what Jorah has reported, things are tense, but the queen believes they were attacked near the border." I heard his words, but they didn't calm me. The queen was no fool. She had to know the truth.

Evren had told me she would stop at nothing until she got me back, and I feared what that nothing would entail. What would she do to Evren if she found out? If she suspected? Would she kill the son of her husband, of her king, if she believed him a traitor?

I knew the answer deep in my gut, and my magic swirled and writhed inside of me, begging for me to let it out, to go after him, to save my mate. But I pushed it down inch by inch as I tried to control my breathing.

"When is he to return?"

"I don't know." Sorin shook his head, and I noted the dark circles under his eyes.

"Any word for us?" Thalia crossed her arms as she studied the captain in front of her.

"Stay down. Stay quiet." Sorin shrugged his shoulders as if that didn't drive him mad, but he rubbed his hand over his eyebrows as he delivered Evren's order. "Evren wants no movement that can tip the queen off on what is happening."

"What is happening?" I looked back and forth between the two of them. I felt so lost, so far on the outside looking in.

"If the queen finds out, if she knows that Evren not only has you but knows of the prophecy, she shall kill us all."

"The queen doesn't know that Evren knows of the prophecy?" As soon as they heard my question, they looked to one another and Thalia wrinkled her brow.

"No." Sorin shook his head, and I watched as his hand tapped against his dagger mindlessly. "The queen thinks it's her best-kept secret. If she had any idea that Evren knew, she would destroy him before he was even able to open his mouth to defend himself. The son of her king be damned. The two of you are the key to the prophecy. The queen needs your hand or Evren's head."

Terror like I never felt before coursed through me, and my magic raged, begging for me to let it out. Uncontrollable, angry, scared. "Then why would he go back there? Why would he do this?"

"Because he's trying to save his people. To save you." Sorin watched me carefully, and I wondered if he could see the magic writhing inside me. "You have no idea what it used to be like. The king may sit on the biggest throne, but it is Queen Kaida who rules. The queen and that fucking son of hers will ruin the whole damn world if we allow them."

"Can you feel your magic now?"

I turned to face Thalia, and she was staring down at my hands. I followed her gaze and watched as trickles of black smoke left my fingers.

"I can't control it." I could hear the irritation, the fear in my own voice.

"It's harder to control when your emotions are high." She moved in front of me and laid her hands against mine. "When you're angry, fearful, or even aroused, your magic will flare inside of you. It is up to you whether you use it or not."

Sorin moved closer to us, but I didn't pull my hands away from Thalia.

"I'm going to leave you two to it." The cockiness was gone from his voice, and my anger only spurred my magic on. If this captain of Evren's guard was so fearful for his prince, his friend, then why didn't he stop him? Why didn't he tell his friend that this was the wrong thing to do?

But I didn't say any of those questions aloud. I held them in and let them twist inside of me with my magic.

Sorin leaned forward, pressing a gentle kiss to Thalia's fore-head, and her eyes fluttered shut before opening again to stare straight ahead at me. Neither one of us watched as he left the courtyard. He simply disappeared, but I was too busy fighting the swarm happening inside of me to care.

Questioning his loyalty, of what they were allowing their prince do, wouldn't help me calm the magic inside me or the fear.

"The first thing you should learn is how to use your emotions to control your power." Thalia lifted her hand and pressed her palm against mine. I jolted back when I felt her power mix with my own. I looked between us, and the most beautiful shade of blue wrapped around my black magic in a caress.

"Why is your... why is your magic blue?"

Thalia cocked her head as she stared down at her magic, and I knew she was thinking about her words carefully. "Everyone's magic has an aura, but most people's magic those stay inside of them. It is rare for someone's magic to escape them like yours or Evren's or even mine." She lifted her fingers and ran them through the smoke between us. "It takes an effort for me to push my magic out of me like this. It's a strain. But it appears to come from you so naturally.

"I've only used my magic a few times." I clenched my hands into fists and tried to pull my smoke back into myself, but it didn't listen. "Each time was when I was fearful or angry. I have no idea what my magic is like otherwise."

"Evren's magic is similar." Thalia took a step back and pulled the blue smoke back into herself before lifting her hand in a gentle motion and knocking me on my ass.

My breath was knocked from my lungs as I hit the ground, and I looked up at her like she had lost her mind. "What was that for?"

"My magic is controlled from here." She pressed her hand against her stomach. "I reach deep inside myself, and I can pull the magic I want. I control it, master it, but Evren's is different."

"What do you mean?"

I dusted off my hands as I sat up and stared at her.

"Evren's magic is more volatile. It's strong, stronger than I've ever seen before, and sometimes hard to control. He is wary of the magic that lies inside of him, and rightfully so. Your magic feels the same to me. The best thing you can do is learn to control it."

My magic stopped inside of me as if watching her, assessing the words she was saying, and I hated how right she was. I had never experienced this kind of magic before, but everything about my magic felt uncontrollable.

It was as angry as I was.

"Show me how."

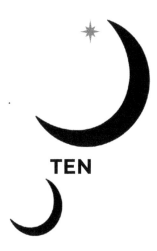

TEN

"This is a bad idea." I pulled on the brand-new pair of boots Thalia had brought to Evren's room and ran my fingers over the supple leather.

"It's just one night." Thalia leaned against the wall as she watched me dress. "You've been training hard. It will be nice to take a little break."

She was right. We had been training to the point my muscles felt like they were going to give out, and most nights I felt like doing nothing more than sleeping. But tonight, I had planned on laying down and reading the book she had given me. A book I hadn't even turned a page on yet because she had kept me so busy.

But I couldn't deny that I did feel stronger both physically and with my magic. Even now just standing here talking to Thalia, I felt more in control of my magic. Whatever Thalia was doing was working, and I was grateful for her because time seemed to be dragging by with every minute that Evren was gone. She knew it too, and she had been doing her best to keep me busy.

But guilt still plagued me as everyone went on with their lives while he was risking his.

"Fine. One night." I held my finger up in her direction. "One drink, then I'm coming back to my room."

"Evren's room." Thalia smirked.

I rolled my eyes and pulled Evren's black shirt over my head and tucked it into my trousers. She knew it belonged to him, but she didn't tease me about it. I wondered if she knew how badly I needed this small connection to him even when I shouldn't. I turned away from her as I tucked the crescent moon necklace into my breasts and shook out my hair.

"Okay. Let's get this over with."

Thalia opened the door and waved me out. "Don't ruin our fun. Sorin will be with us, and I promise we'll have a good time."

"What exactly is going on with you and Sorin anyway?" I looked over at her, and she fidgeted with her hair until it was partly shielding her face. "Are you two having sex?"

Thalia swatted my arm and shushed me.

"Ow!" I laughed as her eyes widened.

"Would you be quiet?" Thalia looked up and down the hall, but there was no one around us. "No. I am not fucking the captain."

"So, what?" I rubbed at the spot where she had just hit. "You're trying to tell me this is all just built-up tension between the two of you?"

Thalia snorted out a laugh. "Something like that."

I grinned as we finally made our way to the entry. Sorin was standing near the door talking to a few of his guards, but his gaze landed on Thalia as soon as we came into view. She was wearing her normal trousers and shirt, but they fit to her body like a second skin. If that girl carried a weapon, I had no idea where she hid it.

A wicked smile appeared on Sorin's face as he looked back and forth between us. "Are you two ready?"

"I'm not exactly sure what I should be ready for," I said without meeting his gaze.

He laughed before dismissing his men with a small nod. "You've been in the Blood kingdom for almost a week, and you haven't left your room unless it's to train or eat. If you're going to be a part of this kingdom, you need to actually experience it."

My gut hardened and my magic flared inside of me, but I tried to focus on calming myself, pulling it back into the center of my chest just as Thalia had taught me. He spoke so easily about me becoming part of this kingdom. "I don't know that I want to be a part of this kingdom."

It was the truth. I didn't know what I was doing. I couldn't make sense of what I wanted. The thought of leaving hadn't run through my mind because I couldn't imagine surviving in a world where I didn't know if Evren was okay.

Sorin's smile fell as my words sobered him up for a moment, but he quickly recovered.

"You know Evren isn't the only thing this kingdom has to offer." He wrapped his arm around mine and pulled me to the door. "Not only do we have extraordinarily handsome captains, but we also make amazing wine."

"You're quite full of yourself, aren't you?"

Thalia snorted from my other side, but Sorin only grinned.

"It's not being full of yourself when it's the truth." He winked at me as we stepped through the door.

The sun was already sinking, and dusk was replacing its light.

"Come on." Sorin tugged me forward, until I had no choice but to keep up with him. "What would you like to see first?"

Everything. The answer was on the tip of my tongue. I wanted to see all this kingdom had to offer. But at the same time, I wanted to see it with Evren. Even through my anger, I knew that this kingdom was his world. It was special to him, and I felt guilty for seeing any of it without him by my side.

"I don't know." I shook my head. "You two decide."

Thalia and Sorin leaned forward and looked at one another, and both grinned at the same time. That should've worried me, but I couldn't get the small thrill to leave my gut.

"The Olde Vine," they both said at the exact same moment and laughed softly. I had no idea what The Olde Vine was, but I had a feeling for the two of them to like it so much, it probably wasn't the most respectful place in the kingdom.

Sorin continued to lead me through the street, and I smiled at all the people who were bustling down the cobblestone road. The Blood kingdom was alive with street sellers and performers and people falling in and out of pubs. There was a laughter that carried onto the streets, a vivaciousness that couldn't be hidden, and my marks buzzed under my skin as I took it all in. They were all watching us as we walked, and I fidgeted with my shirt to try to hide my insecurity.

"Do they know who I am?" I said softly to Sorin, and he smiled down at me.

"Of course, they do."

Just at that moment, an elderly man crossed our path, and when his gaze connected with mine, he faltered for a second. My gut turned, worry fueling me, but the man simply bowed his head as if he was showing me respect. This man, who I could only assume was a vampyre, was showing respect to the Starblessed girl who hadn't earned it.

"Hi, Rhion." Thalia stepped forward and wrapped her arms around the man, and he let out a small chuckle.

"Thalia, my girl. I thought they were never to let you out of that castle." A smile beamed across his face.

"You know me." She grinned at him before she pulled back an arm's length to look over his aging face. "Work, work, work, then I play."

The old man laughed, his chuckle aged and full of spirit. "If only I was about two hundred years younger." His hands squeezed against her arms, and I could see the amusement lighting up her eyes. "I would've stolen you away from this captain back there."

"The captain would have to manage to land me himself for that."

The old man laughed hearty and full, and I couldn't help joining him. Sorin scoffed, even as he fought a grin. "I'll have you know, Rhion, that I'm the most charming guy in this kingdom. Thalia is just a hard one to crack."

Thalia rolled her eyes, and the old man squeezed her tighter. "Maybe you aren't as charming as you think." He winked at her, and she let out a small laugh. "I seem to charm her more than you do, and I'm nothing but an old man."

"You got that right." Thalia leaned forward and pressed a soft kiss against the man's cheek, and he beamed with pride.

"We're headed to The Olde Vine. Would you like to join us?" Thalia's voice was soft as she squeezed his hand in hers, and a little bit of that hard exterior that she always held up cracked before me.

It was such an odd feeling to experience this man, this vampyre, interact so freely with Thalia. I had already seen it with those inside the castle, but this was different. This vampyre was the exact thing I had been taught to fear, but I didn't feel an ounce of unease as I looked at him.

"No. No." The man held up his hands in laughter. "You all go and have fun. This old man needs to get some sleep. Plus, handsome over there won't stand a chance if I'm around."

Thalia laughed as she placed another kiss on his cheek before we said our goodbyes and continued down the road.

"How old is he?" I asked Thalia, and she wrinkled her brow.

"Several hundred years. I don't know exactly."

Chill bumps ran along my arms. I had always been told of

vampyre's immortality, but I hadn't given it much thought until that moment. "And how old is Evren?"

She swallowed hard, and she hesitated before finally answering me. "Just over a century."

"Oh my gods." I pressed my hand to my chest. I knew that Evren was older than me, but I didn't think he was that much older. I never would have fathomed it.

"Don't freak out." She grabbed my hand and pulled me closer to her. "Starblessed live a lot longer than normal humans."

"What?" My chest tightened, but there was an edge of relief that I felt as well. Why did I care how long I would live in comparison to my mate when I wasn't meant to care for him at all?

"Did you not read any of the book I gave you?" She rolled her eyes.

"I did, but I hadn't got to that part." I crossed my arms and searched her face. "Wait, how old are you?"

"A lot older than you." She laughed and tightened her hand in mine.

People were watching us. Everywhere we went their eyes slid in our direction, but none of them were judging, calculating, or cruel. Everyone who looked upon Sorin and Thalia did so with admiration, and those who looked upon me did so with respect or maybe curiosity. They lowered their heads briefly, but their eyes never left me.

"These people"—Sorin nodded toward all the people that surrounded us—"love their prince. And as his mate, they will love you too."

"They know I'm his mate?"

"I don't know how much you know about vampyres, Adara. But we have a keen sense of smell, and my boy Evren made sure to mark you in every possible way before he left you here."

I couldn't stop the blush from creeping up my neck and into my face. Oh my gods.

"Having sex with someone does not make them your mate."

Sorin snorted and his eyes widened at my words. "That's not what I meant." He looked me up and down, and my blush only worsened. "His scent is wrapped around you. His magic. Your mating bond is strong and pure and unmistakable. The fact that you two fucked before he left is news to me, Adara."

My gaze swung to Thalia, and she held up her hands. "I told you your secrets were your own. I didn't realize you were just going to tell them to everyone."

"Come on." Sorin laughed and waved us forward. "We're here."

Here was a small pub that was covered in vines and ancient stones. The door was curved and carved beautifully, but it was the boisterous laughter from inside that drew me in.

We walked into the pub, and everyone cheered when they saw Sorin. "You come here often?"

Thalia laughed at my question. "He has to come somewhere to drown all his misery when his charms fail to get in my trousers."

I laughed, and Sorin grinned. Despite what they said or how they acted, they looked at one another often and the smiles on their faces always reached their eyes.

"By the way she talks, you'd think she hates me. Truly, she's just waiting to get courted properly."

"In your dreams." Thalia pulled out a chair at a small table, and the three of us sat down. The bartender, a young girl with beautiful curly hair and some of the darkest eyes I had ever seen, came to our table almost immediately, and she grinned at my two companions. "How are you?"

"Were good, Lis. How are you?"

"Busy." The girl laughed and just as she did, another round of laughter rang out around us. The pub was packed to the brim with men and women, and every one of them seemed happy to be there.

"I can see that." Sorin smiled as a man walked by and patted him on the shoulder. "Do you think we can get three glasses of wine?"

"Of course." She nodded and wiped her hands on her cream apron. "Whose tab are we putting this on? Yours or Thalia's?" She grinned as she looked back and forth between them, but they were too busy looking at each other with smirks on their faces to notice.

"Evren's." Sorin wrapped his arm around me and pulled my chair closer to him, the sound of wood scraping against the floor ringing out through the pub. "We are out with his mate. He might as well pay. Don't you think?"

I opened my mouth in shock, but Lis only laughed as if this was the best idea she ever heard. "Of course, it's nice to meet you, Starblessed. I've heard so much about you already."

I was caught off guard by her, but I quickly recovered. "It's nice to meet you as well, but please call me Adara and please don't get any information from the wild ideas these two share with you." I hiked my thumbs in the direction of my two companions and both of them started with laughter.

"Don't worry, Adara." She shook her head. "I haven't trusted these two in years."

I liked her instantly. She smiled one last time before she walked away from the table and back toward the bar to get our wine.

"I cannot believe you just did that."

"Why not?" Thalia nodded and tapped her fingers against the table. "The prince owes me."

They both smiled, and I wondered if Evren would have been the same if he were here. I wanted to see him like this, to see him carefree with his friends, to see him living life.

It was all I could think about. My desperation for him to be here, to see him alive and not in danger. How could I hate someone if I cared so deeply for their safety? When they were so willing to risk so much because they cared for my own?

"Here you go." Lis set the wine down in front of us, and I reached out quickly for a glass.

I brought the deep amber liquid to my mouth, and a small moan left my lips at the taste. "Oh my gods. This is divine."

"I told you." Sorin lifted his own drink and brought it to his lips.

I watched the people around us. Each one of them were laughing and singing and enjoying their night. I slowly sipped my wine as I watched them and thought about how fearful I had been of this kingdom. I thought of all the histories I had been told and how none of them appeared to be true. That was a hard truth to face. Everything that I thought I knew was wrong.

Was everything my mother had ever told me a lie?

I was still contemplating that thought, thinking of how foolish I felt, when a large man stopped at our table. His beard was full and his smile even fuller, and he was staring straight at me.

"Come on, you." He waved me up from the table. "You can't just stay here with these two bores. Let me spin you around the floor."

Sorin laughed, and I looked back and forth between them as a smile formed on my lips.

"Since when did you learn to dance? Last time I checked you had nothing but two left feet." Sorin leaned back and rested his arm along the back of my chair.

The man rolled his eyes before winking at me. There was a softness to his smile, so I scooted out my chair and avoided looking at Sorin when his gaze flew to me. Instead, I put my hand to the man's outstretched one. "Let's prove him wrong."

The man chuckled and pulled me into him, his grip strong, and I laughed and almost tripped over my own two feet. But he pulled me toward the dance floor and spun me around quickly until I had no choice but to stop overthinking and just enjoy dancing with this man.

"Two left feet." He scoffed. "That boy doesn't have a damn clue what he's talking about." He took my hand in his and spun me out from his body before spinning me back quickly. My head was dizzy and my smile full, and I busted out in laughter as my chest slammed back into his. He wasn't a good dancer. Sorin was right about that, but gods he was fun.

"He does seem pretty full of it." I laughed.

"I'd say, but he's got that face and all that hair." He waved his hand in Sorin's direction. "It gets him away with far too much."

"I'd say that he and Prince Evren have that in common."

He chuckled and almost stepped on my toes. "Our poor prince. He's going to have his hands full with you."

"You don't think the prince can handle me?"

The man spun me around again, and I couldn't tell if it was the wine or the dancing that was getting to my head.

"Oh, I'm sure he'll handle you just fine. But I have a feeling it'll be fun watching you test him every step of the way."

I smiled, but this was foolish. Talking to these people like my presence in their kingdom was permanent. He spoke like I belonged to Evren, like I belonged to him and no one else.

That was foolish.

The pressure to make a choice about my future was heavier than ever. What was I going to do? I knew that I would never return to Gavril. No matter what they did or threatened. I would never go back to the fae kingdom, but would I so willingly become a part of Evren's?

I had barely seen Queen Veda since we had arrived, but I didn't trust her. She had given me every reason not to.

When her men attacked us in the woods, any chance of me trusting her was lost, and I didn't know how controlled Evren was by his mother. I knew he was nothing like Gavril, I knew that deep in my gut, but I would be a fool to blindly believe that he would have chosen me had I not been the perfect pawn in his game. Evren had already proved to me that he was capable of betraying me, and I wouldn't be foolish enough not to remember that.

"Oh no." The man pulled me back into him and wrapped his large hand around my back. "I'm sorry. I didn't mean to upset you."

"You didn't." I shook my head quickly, and I hoped to reassure him. "I was just thinking."

"Well, if it helps at all, I want you to know that our prince can take care of you because he was born to do so. He is your mate, and he is our savior. Don't underestimate the boy."

I let his words sink in, to fill me with everything I needed to hear, and I grinned as I tried to drown out the intrusive thoughts that I wanted to stop.

I didn't have to worry about this tonight. To make decisions. All I could do was have fun with these people and let my fear for Evren hide in my gut as I pushed it down. He was my mate, and I didn't know how harshly that truth would affect my life.

"All right. It's my turn to cut in."

The man swung me back into him and tugged me against his chest as I laughed. Sorin reached out his hand, but he hardly seemed to notice.

"Can't you see me and the girl are having fun?" He winked down at me, and I couldn't stop myself from laughing.

"Take turns before I'm forced to go over there and ask your wife for a dance."

The man laughed, and I looked around trying to figure out who his wife was. Whoever she was, I imagined her life was full of love and laughter, and for a small moment, I was envious of her.

"Fine." He slipped my hand out to his and motioned me toward Sorin. "She's all yours for now."

I let my hands slip into Sorin's, and he pulled me close to him as the music rang out around the pub.

"You've got some big shoes to fill." I laughed as I watched the man walk away. "I can't remember having that much fun while dancing ever."

"Well, that's because you haven't danced with me before." Sorin grinned, and he was so handsome. His brown hair was pushed back out of his face and tied at the back of his head with a small leather strap. Even in the middle of this pub, holding me in his arms with that grin on his face, he still looked every bit the warrior that he was.

Sorin moved us around the floor quickly, spinning our bodies in time with the music, and I laughed when my head felt so dizzy that I thought I was going to fall.

"I wish Evren were here." The words slipped past my lips, and my smile faltered.

Sorin slowed us down only minutely, but he lifted his hand and pushed my wild hair out of my face. "Me too." He studied me with a soft smile that didn't quite reach his eyes. "You have no idea how much."

He spun me around again, and I tried not to let myself think about it. Think about how Evren would spin me around the floor. How he would drive me crazy with want just by the simple touch of his fingers. But it was impossible not to. Even from miles away, he invaded every part of me.

"He'll come back." His words were soft and meant for me alone. But they rang inside of me, sinking deep in my bones, and my magic spurred me to life at the promise. A promise that I was desperate to come true.

And that desperation made me feel more vulnerable than ever. Because I couldn't deny he was all I wanted in that moment.

Because I was alone in this kingdom, and I had been alone in the kingdom before this, and all I ever had was Evren. Even before I realized it, it was always him. Even through his betrayal, it was him.

"Are you two going to make me drink all this wine alone?" Thalia called out to us as she held a bottle of wine in her hands. I laughed and pulled myself away from Sorin as I made my way back to the table. Wine was exactly what I needed. I needed it to help drown my thoughts and the feelings that were invading me.

"I'll have another glass."

Thalia smiled before popping the cork and filling my glass to the brim.

"Tonight, we have fun. Then tomorrow we'll work.

ELEVEN

I could feel the rolling of last night's drink churning in my empty stomach.

"Again!" Thalia called out, and her voice echoed inside my head.

"I need a break."

Thalia snorted, and I could feel her irritation with me without even looking at her face. "If I had known you couldn't handle your drink, I would've never given you so much wine."

"Well, now you know." I huffed out a tired·breath and prayed for my head to quit pounding.

"It doesn't matter." She raised her hands and waited for me to get back in my stance. "If you're attacked, they aren't going to make sure you've recovered from a night of drinking and dancing before they finish the job."

She was right. Of course she was, but it didn't matter. All I could think about was how badly I wanted was go back to Evren's room and take a long nap.

But there wasn't a chance in hell Thalia was going to let that happen.

"Fine." I widened my stance and tried to focus on my

breathing as I waited for her move as she lunged at me. This time, I was anticipating it. I shot to the left, and only felt the wind from her movements. She didn't land a single touch.

"Better." She nodded her head as I wiped sweat from my brow. "Again."

We did that over and over again, her changing up her movements every time, and me trying to anticipate what she would do. She landed at least ninety percent of her hits, and I was aching all over.

I feared that she wouldn't stop until I was puking, and I breathed a sigh of relief when Sorin rushed out onto the courtyard. I was looking forward to his cocky banter, because at least I could catch my breath.

I pressed my hands against my knees and bent at my waist as I swallowed breath after breath. But my head snapped up at the sound of Thalia's worried voice.

"What's wrong?"

I looked to Sorin, and he was taking short, shallow breaths, and his eyes were wide with panic.

"It's Evren." His hand was held firmly against his dagger. "We just received word from Jorah that Queen Kaida knows of his treason."

Everything stopped. Everything but my raging panic. "What does that mean?" My magic swirled inside of me, and I feared that even though I'd been training to control it, I wouldn't be able to right now.

Sorin simply shook his head, and it angered me. Fueled me.

"What does that mean?" I growled, and his gaze snapped to me.

"I don't know." His voice shook with emotion he tried to hide.

I shouldn't have been angry with him, but I couldn't stop the way it was crawling inside of me. The anger and the fear. It was taking over, and Sorin was the one bringing it out in me even though he wasn't doing it purposefully.

I had no control.

"Where is my mate?" I snapped as inky black magic trailed from my fingers, and I watched as Sorin looked down and took it all in. But I lost the ability to pull it back. My heart raced as my power felt so uncontrollable. Evren was in trouble, and I couldn't just stand here and work on my breathing while attempting to control my magic. I didn't need to do anything but get to him.

"He's missing." Sorin delivered the line like it didn't pierce through my entire soul and rock my entire being.

He was missing. My mate was missing and that could only mean…

I shook my head as I tried to shake off my fear. I couldn't go there. I couldn't let myself begin to fathom what that could mean.

"I'm going after him," I growled out through clenched teeth.

I moved to the side of the courtyard and grabbed my dagger before either of them could stop me. I heard Sorin curse under his breath, but I didn't allow it to slow me down. I needed to get to Evren, and no one was going to stand in my way.

I rushed through the door, back into the castle, and my hands trembled. I didn't know what I was going to do, but I knew that I couldn't just sit here. He was their prince, but he was my mate, and I wouldn't allow us to sit here while only the gods knew what was happening to him.

I pushed down the hall but stopped short when Queen Veda moved into my path. Her dark hair was a mess as if she had been running her fingers through it, and two of her guards stood at her back at full attention.

"I'm taking it you've heard the news of Evren." Her voice was so controlled, so calm, and I hated it.

"I have." I went to move past her, but she sidestepped and blocked me.

"You can't go after him."

I met her gaze, and I held it there for a long time. She wasn't my queen. I wasn't hers to rule.

"I am." My voice held conviction, and I wondered if she could taste my power as it thrummed through every part of me. "You can't stop me."

"You are the Starblessed that has been prophesied, Adara. Evren would kill me if I allowed you to fall back into the hands of his brother by not protecting you."

"And I will kill you if you don't move out of my way." I felt someone at my back at that moment, and my anger rose as I expected them to stop me. But Thalia did no such thing. She simply stood behind me, her chest pressed against my back, and stayed silent.

"I am not your enemy, Adara." The queen looked past me and her brow furrowed. "But I will lock you away until he's found if you force my hand."

Thalia moved even closer to me, her chest pressing fully against my back, and even though I knew she had been a part of this kingdom for much longer than she knew me, every part of me knew that she would choose me if the queen forced her to.

If it came down to the queen or me, Thalia would choose me.

"That won't be necessary." Sorin moved to my side, and he smiled at the queen. "Me and my men are heading out within the hour to search for our prince, and Adara and Thalia will stay back in case there is any news."

My gaze shot to him, and I wanted to tell him that he was crazy. I wanted to demand that he take me with him, but his eyes widened and his jaw ticked. It wasn't an order. It was a silent plea for me to listen.

And I looked back to the queen but kept my mouth shut.

She watched me carefully with her lips pressed together in a thin line. "You have to handle things carefully, Sorin." She finally looked away from me. "We don't know what all Queen Kaida knows."

"Of course, Your Majesty." Sorin bowed his head slightly as Thalia took my hand in hers. "And neither of you shall leave the palace."

I could feel Thalia's magic flare against my own in my palm. Her jaw clenched and her posture was stiff as she held me near her. She didn't look to the queen when she replied. Instead, her gaze held steady with Sorin's. Her face paled and her hand shook in mine. "We will be here for whatever you need."

"It's settled then." The queen looked between the three of us before Thalia tightened her hand in mine. "Sorin, bring back my son."

Sorin nodded before bowing once more, and I pulled Thalia forward and away from the queen. I knew that Evren trusted her. She was his mother, but I couldn't force the same feeling. My trust for her remained lacking.

But right now, we both wanted the same thing. We wanted Evren home safely, and I couldn't do something foolish that would get in the way of that.

TWELVE

I typically took dinner alone in Evren's room, but Thalia had refused to leave me on my own ever since the news of Evren arrived.

I didn't know if it was simply because she was worried about me or because she feared what I would do, but either way, she hadn't left my side.

Thalia was sitting across from me at Evren's little desk, and I had no idea where she found the chair that she had pulled into his room.

"You're like a mother hen." I tore a piece of bread and dipped it into the stew Mina had brought in.

Thalia simply shrugged and her gaze held firm to mine. "I just want to make sure you're okay. "

"I'm fine." It was a lie and her presence spoke to her disbelief of my proclamation. It had been two days since Evren had went missing. Two days since we had any word from Jorah or Sorin about what was going on, and everything inside me was begging me not to listen to their demands that I stay in the kingdom.

But I was far more fearful of losing Evren than I was of any of their wrath.

He had been gone for far too long, and I wasn't sure how much more I could take.

"No, you're not." She shook her head and took a sip of her wine. "How could you be?" We don't know they're okay. Not Evren, Jorah, or Sorin."

I tucked my knee up against my chest and studied my friend. I was dressed in nothing but one of Evren's shirts, but I hadn't expected the company. I was planning to crawl in bed and try to sleep away my rising fear before Thalia had knock at my door.

I opened my mouth to answer her, but as soon as I did the door to Evren's room burst open. Both Thalia and I jumped to our feet and my magic swirled around my hands as panic took over.

But it was Mina who stood at the door with her hands against her chest.

"What is it?" I asked, breathlessly.

"It's Evren. He's back."

Before I could think better of it, I tore from the room. I had no idea where I was going or where he would be, but I couldn't stop to think. I simply took off, my bare feet slapping against the ground, and I couldn't control a single emotion that was racing through me. I could hear Thalia behind me, and everything about her felt as uncontrollable as I did. Evren may not have been her mate, but he was her prince, and more importantly, her friend.

I skidded to a halt when I hit the main entry of the castle, and I watched in horror as Queen Veda leaned over her son who was propped up against the stone wall. His face looked sickly and drained of life, and Queen Veda cursed as she pulled his bloody shirt away from his skin to look beneath it. Sorin paced around the room with blood staining his hands, but he looked up as soon as he saw us. "Adara, he needs you."

I looked past him to Evren, and I could feel my fear as if it had become alive within me. I hesitated, crippled with raging emotions, but Thalia moved past me quickly. She dropped her knees beside Evren as my stomach turned to panic and guilt.

I hesitated, and Thalia watched me for only a moment before she rolled up the sleeve of her shirt. She was giving me a choice, but when she saw me stutter in my indecision, she took things into her own hands. She was going to save his life. He was going to feed from her, and it would save him.

I should have let it happen. Evren needed her in that moment, and I should have kept my mouth shut. But he was my mate. My magic rolled around my hands violently, and I knew I couldn't sit here and simply watch as he fed from someone else. I cursed under my breath as I tried to shove down the fear that was clawing at every inch of me. I pushed forward and dropped to my knees beside Thalia. Evren's eyes connected with mine, and his gaze softened as he sagged further against the wall.

"Princess." The word was soft and barely heard, but it rang through me as if he had screamed it.

This was my mate, and I was his.

I pushed the sleeve up my arm that held my black mark with trails of stars within it and held my wrist out toward him.

"Take from me."

His gaze trailed over my face, before he slowly lifted his shaking hand and followed its path. I shivered under his touch and my heart raced in my chest. *This was my mate.*

"Are you okay?" His voice was thick and quiet.

I choked on a laugh at his question and tears sprang to my eyes. *Was I okay? Was he insane?*

"Do not worry about me." I pressed my hand against his where it was resting against my neck. "Take from me, Evren."

His eyes shuttered, and I wondered what all he had been through. Who had hurt him like this? Was it the queen? Was it his brother?

"You don't have to do this." He shook his head softly, and even that took an effort.

"What are you talking about? Take from me." I begged, knowing that every second that passed, he remained in pain. He remained at risk.

"I promised you I would never be like him." His gaze was soft and pleading, and I knew what he meant. He didn't want to be like his brother, taking from me against my will, but he didn't understand. "You don't have to do this."

"He can take from me." Thalia looked at me softly, and I knew she only said it because she knew how badly I warred with myself. But there wasn't an ounce of indecision left in me. This was my mate, and it would be me who saved him. "It's all right, Adara."

I shook my head as I stared down at him. "I am your mate, Evren, and you will feed from me."

His gaze sparked in surprise before his lips parted and his hand tightened against my neck. My stomach clinched tight, and my breath caught in my throat, but I didn't have time to steady myself before Evren lifted my wrist to his mouth. He sank his teeth into my skin. I closed my eyes, and I forgot about everyone else around us. This was Evren and me, and even though he was hurt, he was here, and he was safe. The queen couldn't touch him here. Neither could Gavril, and I reminded myself of that fact over and over again.

His magic surged through me as he drank, and my body was lit afire as every inch of me became alive within his touch. I was still so angry with him, but I couldn't deny my want. I couldn't recognize that pain that blared through me with his feeding when I was so lost in my desire and relief. But I forced myself to cling on to my anger because without it I knew I would be hurt. Seeing him like this now gripped my chest in a vise, and I couldn't imagine how much worse it could be if I let myself fall into him completely.

He drank long and hard, and I could feel myself draining. But as every drop drained from me and into him, my body ached deeper and deeper, and I couldn't remember why I wasn't supposed to want him.

"That's enough, Evren." I couldn't make out who said it, but they were probably right. But I didn't want him to stop. I never wanted him to stop. I wanted to live in this moment, in this feeling of ache and want, and I wanted no one to stop him.

He pulled his teeth from my skin slowly, and I gasped for breath as his magic pulled away.

More. The thought rang out in my head, and I couldn't be sure that I didn't say it aloud. But it was all I could think. *More. More. More.* He was my mate, and I wanted more.

I blinked my eyes open, and Evren was gripping both of my arms. He pulled me into him, and I had no choice but to allow it. Pressing against his chest, I took a deep breath of the scent of him. My nose buried in his neck, and I clung to him hard. Refusing to let go.

"Princess," Evren whispered my name, and his voice sounded so much clearer, stronger than before.

I didn't answer him. I simply snuggled in harder against his chest and tightened my arms around him.

"It's okay." He ran his hands over my hair, and I could feel myself trembling against him. "Everything is going to be okay."

My legs were straddled around his waist, and I could hear the murmur of voices behind us, but I couldn't bring myself to care. In that moment, it didn't matter what any of them thought of me. All I could think about was him and the deep ache coursing inside of me.

"I need you." I let the plea fall from my lips that still pressed against his neck.

Evren groaned but didn't try to stop me. I pressed my lips to his neck and his hand ran down the length of my spine. My marks were aflame along my skin, and the ache between my thighs was overpowering.

I could focus on nothing else.

"I need you all to leave." He growled, but I was far too bewitched by my want for him to know if they listened.

"Evren, I need you." My voice sounded panicked and desperate, but I couldn't bring myself to care. Every breath of it was the truth.

"You hate me," he whispered, and I forced myself to sit up and stare into his dark, tired eyes. "If I gave you what you wanted right now, you would hate me."

Part of me knew he was probably right, but that didn't stop the anger from surging inside of me. I needed him. Needed him more than I had ever needed anything in my life, and he was going to deny me.

"Agree to be mine. Agree to marry me, and I'll give you everything you want."

My marks felt like they were burning me alive at his words. He had just gotten back. He had been insanely injured, and he was worried about marrying me?

"I don't want to be a part of your games." I shook my head. "I don't want to be the answer to the prophecy."

Evren ran his fingers over my face, pushing my hair back before gripping the back my neck. "This has nothing to do with that. Marry me because you want to. Marry me because I'm your mate."

I pushed against his chest, frustration and want making me feel insane. It was on the tip of my tongue to tell him yes. To tell him that I would give him anything he wanted from me, but I couldn't do that. Not now. Not when there were still so many unanswered questions between us.

"I'm glad you're back." I pushed farther away from him and realized in that moment that I was sitting across his lap wearing only his shirt. There were still others around us, but most had listened and left the room. But Queen Veda was watching us, her gaze bouncing back and forth between us, calculating our every touch, and I couldn't stand the way my stomach tightened in worry.

"Evren, we should talk."

Evren looked up at his mother, and I dug my fingers into his chest. I didn't want to give him up to her. Not even for a second, and his gaze flew back to mine as if he, too, couldn't fathom us leaving one another.

"It can wait." He lifted his hand slowly and pressed it against my cheek.

"We both know it can't." The queen's voice was firm and left no room for argument.

He stared at me for a long moment before he slipped my hand into his and lifted my wrist against his mouth. He pressed a gentle kiss along the sensitive skin before he whispered his next words. "I'll come find you shortly. Wait for me."

I didn't say a word. I simply climbed from his lap and straightened his shirt over my body. Thalia was there in an instant. She reached out for me, ready to offer her strength in my moment of weakness. Evren looked back and forth between us before his mother called his name again.

"Let's get back to your room," Thalia spoke softly, and I nodded in agreement. I wanted to be anywhere but here. Evren was back. He was safe, and I shouldn't have been desperate to hold on to him and make sure that no one else could touch him, but I was. The frenzy I felt was churning in my magic, and every inch of me ached to reach out for him.

"Adara," Thalia said my name more firmly, and I finally looked away from the prince and looked up at her. "We'll find Evren later. We should get you dressed."

I let her pull me away from him, each step feeling like torture, and as we made our way back to Evren's room, I couldn't breathe.

"Not here." I quickly shook my head. This was Evren's room, his space, and I had been invading it without his permission.

Tahlia nodded as if she understood and motioned toward my door. "Go ahead. I'll clean up our mess from earlier."

I hadn't even thought of that. I hadn't thought of what it would look like when he walked in and saw all of my things.

"Okay." I nodded and walked backward until my trembling fingers pressed against my door. I pushed inside and closed the door securely behind me, and only then did I allow myself to fall to my knees and thank the gods that Evren was back.

THIRTEEN

The palace was eerily quiet, but my worry was roaring against the walls of my room. It had been hours since I left Evren. Hours since his mother had called for him.

And my body had been burning for him ever since. I laid back in bed and slammed my head against the pillow in a huff. Everywhere the blankets were touching me was too much, every graze against my skin kept me burning, and I felt like I was going to implode.

Evren's magic was still coursing through me. It snaked through my veins, caressing every inch of me, and it was driving me crazy. I lifted my hands and let some of my magic seep from my fingertips. It swirled around the darkness, fueling me, but it did nothing to calm me.

I slammed my hands back down against the bed, and my magic cut off immediately. I prayed to the gods for sleep to claim me. I had been begging ever since I walked into my room, but they were no help to me.

Marry me.

I threw the blankets toward the side of the bed.

Marry me.

His words rolled through me like a storm I was incapable of stopping, and I thought of little else. What would it be like if I just simply gave in to him, gave into everything I wanted but was too afraid to take.

I ran my fingers down my body and gripped the edge of Evren's shirt. The tips of my fingers pressed against the tops of my thighs and a small whimper passed through my lips.

I closed my eyes as I let myself think about what it would be like to be his… what it would be like if I just gave in and allowed him to have whatever part of me he wanted.

I pushed my fingers higher until they grazed over my hips. I imagined they were his. I tried to think about exactly what he would do if it were his hands instead of my own.

I let them slide into my undergarments, and I closed my eyes as I pressed my head back against my pillow. I was already so wet, so turned on from Evren feeding from me hours ago, and my legs clamped together as I ran my finger over my sensitive nub.

"Open them." The sound of Evren's voice had me jumping in shock, and my gaze slammed into his where he was leaning next to my fireplace. I hadn't heard him come in, and I was embarrassed that I was too distracted by my greed to sense him.

"What are you doing in here?"

"I came to find you." His gaze fell to my legs, and I could see his own hunger in his gaze.

"Are you okay?"

"We're not talking about me right now." He ran his hand over the scruff on his jaw, so much longer than the last time I had seen him. "Open your fucking legs, princess."

He wasn't asking me. It was a command, and a moan slipped past my lips at the sound of his voice.

I slowly let my knees fall open, and he groaned at the sight of me. "That's a good girl. Let me see it."

A chill ran down my spine, and I had no idea what I was

doing. But I let my legs fall wide open as I watched him take me in.

"Move your hand. Touch yourself just like you imagine I would."

I slowly moved my fingers, and I clenched my eyes shut as embarrassment and pleasure coursed through me. It didn't matter that he had already seen every part of me. This was different.

"Take them off." Evren's voice sounded closer, and I snapped my eyes open to look at him. He stood at the end of my bed with one hand pressed against the frame. "I want to see you."

I hesitated, and if Evren could see the fear in my eyes, he simply obliterated it with his words. "I've been dying for you, princess. Let me see what's mine."

I pulled my fingers out and hooked my thumbs into the waistband of my undergarments. I slowly slid them down my thighs as he watched, my fingers trembling as I pulled them past my feet and let them fall to the bed beside me. I was completely bare before him in nothing but his shirt that did little to hide my body, and I could barely catch my breath as he watched me.

"Press your thighs into the bed," he instructed me, and I slowly did as he said as a shudder of his power coursed through the room. Even without touching myself, a shot of pleasure rushed through me.

"Show me what you like." He ran his hand over the front of his trousers, and I tried to swallow against the rising emotions inside of me. "Show your mate exactly how you like to be touched."

I pressed my fingers against my sex, and he stalked every single movement with rapt attention as I slowly moved my fingers against the moisture that was coating my nub.

"Taste it."

My gaze shot back to his.

"Put your fingers in your mouth and taste how fucking perfect you are."

I shouldn't have been so aroused by his words, but I couldn't stop myself as I held his gaze and followed his orders. I slipped my fingers into my mouth and closed my lips around them before tasting myself with my tongue.

"I have thought of little else since I left." His hands fisted against the bedpost, and the wood creaked under his grip. "I could concentrate on nothing other than the memory of how sweet you tasted when I pleasured you with my tongue."

I let my fingers slip from my mouth. "Oh gods." I pushed them back through my sex and my body jerked as I met my nub once more.

"That's it, princess. Show me how badly you've missed me. Show me how desperate your body is for your mate."

I let his words encourage me. I simply used my hand and focused on him as he watched me come apart.

I slid my hand lower, sliding a finger inside myself, and Evren let out a curse. "Whose is it, princess? Who does your body belong to? Show me that no other man will ever taste you the way I long to."

My back arched off the bed as my palm pressed against my nub. I pulled my fingers in and out of myself, and I imagined it was him. I imagined that it was him filling me up instead of myself, and my other hand squeezed my breast through his shirt.

"Say it, princess."

"You." The word rushed out of me on a ragged breath. "I belong to you."

"You're fucking right you do." His breathing matched my own, and I looked down to watch him as he pulled his cock from his trousers and started working himself with his hand. "You belong to me, Adara. You are mine and mine alone. Just as I am yours."

I couldn't bring myself to be angry with his words because he was right. No matter how I tried to deny it, I was his.

"Did you sleep in my bed, princess?" His question caught me

off guard, and my hand paused as I looked at him. "Don't you dare fucking stop," he growled, and I whimpered as I started moving again.

I rolled my hips against my hand and watched as he squeezed the tip of his cock in his fist. "I could smell you on my sheets. I tried to lie down tonight, to give you just a moment alone, but you wrapped around me as soon as I got in there and I could think of nothing else. Did you think of me, princess, while you were lying in my bed with your hand buried between your thighs?"

"I always think of you." The confession fell from my lips.

"And I of you." He groaned as his hand moved faster against his cock. "I obsess over the way you say my name and how you try to deny the fact that you're mine. I'm haunted by memories of the way your body feels wrapped around me."

My fingers moved harder and faster, and I was desperate for the feeling I was chasing. My magic stormed inside of me along with his, and they chased it with me.

"I need you." I widened my thighs so he could see how hope-lessly I wanted him. "Please, Evren."

He watched me like a hunter stalking his prey, and I widened them even more. "Marry me."

"What?" I didn't know why he was talking about this right now. I couldn't think of anything other than this feeling coursing through me, teetering on the edge of crashing at any moment. I just needed him to touch me.

"Marry me, and you'll know nothing but pleasure, Adara. Marry me and I promise you'll want for nothing."

My fingers moved harder, and I whimpered against the movement. "I don't need you to be my husband, Evren." My magic flared and the words tasted bitter on my tongue. "I need you to fuck me."

He chuckled softly, but it held no ounce of humor. "And I will. I'll fuck you every possible chance I get. I won't leave a single inch of your body undiscovered once you give yourself to me."

I groaned in frustration and ran my fingers up my neck. I just needed a little more.

"Press more firmly, princess. Imagine your fingers are my own and take your own breath away until you give me what I want. Take your breath away until you find your release against those perfect fucking fingers of yours."

My sex clamped down around my fingers as I took in his words, but I hesitated.

"Do what you're told, princess."

I gasped for breath before I let my fingers dig into my skin. I only used the slightest amount of pressure against my neck, but already, I could feel myself falling.

"That's it." His voice reassured me, and I gasped as I felt his magic slowly snake over my hand.

It pushed down, encouraging me, and my hand trembled beneath it.

"Take it." His voice was gruff with a mixture of his own pleasure and pain. "Take your fucking pleasure, princess."

I choked on a breath as my hand moved harder, and it was only another moment before I could feel it crashing into me. Pleasure, hard and unrelenting, slammed through me, and I didn't stand a chance of holding any part of it back. I screamed out Evren's name, as his magic moved from my hand and ran over my body.

It crept its way over every inch of me, caressing and feeling and leaving chill bumps in its wake.

"You are mine, Adara."

My gaze hit his as his hand moved roughly against himself.

"No one will ever have you again but me. I could feel you in here. Your want for me was palpable, as was your uncertainty. But every bit of it belongs to me."

His power tightened against me, and it shuddered against my

body. Another rush of pleasure shot through me as I watched him come so hard he had to use my bedpost to hold himself up.

We stared at each other for a long moment as both of us tried to catch our breaths, and the reality of what we had just done sank in. The reality of his words.

He tucked himself back in his trousers after cleaning himself up, and he stared straight ahead to where my legs were clamped together.

"Good night, princess." He spoke softly and his gaze held firm against me. His hands fisted in my bedding as his lips parted, but I couldn't make myself form the words to ask him to stay. To beg him to never leave me again.

I had just shown him so much of myself, so much weakness in my want, and I hated how desperately I wanted to give him all of me.

He turned his back to me and walked to the door but hesitated with his hand on the handle.

Before I could think better of it, I told him the only truth I was willing to give. "I could feel you too, you know? The night you left. I knew deep in my gut that something wasn't right."

"That's because you're my mate, Adara. Every part of you is made for me, and it drives me crazy."

"But you still left."

He turned until his gaze could meet my own, and I could feel his magic coiling inside of him.

"Don't make me choose between you and my kingdom, princess. Because I will choose you. Consequences be damned, I will choose you."

I gasped down a breath as my magic sparked to life, and Evren looked to me once more before he opened the door and disappeared into the hall.

FOURTEEN

"I get that you're upset for whatever reason but take a breath." Thalia wiped the sweat from her brow as I shook out my hands. "Your emotions are hindering you."

I wasn't upset. I was confused, and hell, maybe I was angry. I didn't know what to feel.

Evren being back was supposed to fix things, not confuse me more, but all I could think about were the words he had said before he left my room. The words that threw me more than anything else ever could.

He had felt different somehow, the conviction in his words left no room for misunderstanding, but I didn't know if I was ready for the heavy consequences of his choices. He said he would choose me, but would he be making that choice to keep his kingdom safe or because of his feelings for me?

"We need to train." I wiped my sweating hands down my trousers and lined myself back up.

Thalia was trying to teach me how to control myself when not only using my magic but in hand-to-hand combat as well, and it was much harder than I thought it would be.

"Okay, but you don't need to run yourself into the ground to not think about him." She looked toward the doorway, and her mouth tightened in a hard line.

I balled my hands into fists before shaking them out, and I tried to let her words roll off me.

"Don't hold back this time," I told her just before she lunged at me and let a flare of her magic come barreling at my chest.

I lifted my left hand, blocking her magic with my own, but her fist connected with my shoulder before I could stop it.

"Shit," I cursed as I almost lost my balance. My shoulder was already aching from the hit, but it didn't matter. I wasn't ready to stop. "Again."

Thalia nodded once before lining herself back up, and I tried to watch her eyes to see the directions her thoughts were going. But I was wrong. She lunged to the left, her leg kicking out toward me, and I shifted my weight, bracing for her attack, and I completely missed the way her magic slammed into my right side. I hit the ground with a loud grunt and clenched my teeth at the bite of pain in my hip.

"Stop overthinking." Thalia pushed her hair out of her face. "You're not trusting yourself, Adara. You need to take a moment and catch your breath."

I crawled to my knees before pushing back to my stance, and I tried to control the anger that was coursing through me. "I don't need a break."

"Then I do."

I looked up at Thalia because it was the first time she'd ever told me she needed a break. Her eyes were pleading, and she rubbed her hand across her brow.

"I'll take over." I snapped my head in the direction of Evren's voice and watched as he strolled into the courtyard. He was dressed in his usual black attire, and there was no trace of the man who had been attacked. He looked every bit his normal self.

"I don't really think you should be doing any training." I

pressed my hands into my hips as I try to swallow down a breath. "Weren't you the one crumpled on the floor last night?"

Evren smirked as he circled around me and stepped in front of Thalia. "I did a lot of things last night, but miraculously, I've got my energy back."

I tried not to react to his words, but all I could think about was what he looked like at the end of my bed. All I could remember was the feel of his magic against my skin.

"I don't want to train with you."

Evren smirked harder and cocked his head as he looked at me. "It would seem you're all out of choices, considering you've worn Thalia out."

"Where's Sorin?" I looked around the courtyard, but it was only the three of us there. "I would rather finish my training with him."

Evren bared his teeth, and he took a moment before he spoke again.

"I thought we made it clear last night that you are mine. You will train with me."

I heard Thalia let out a snicker under her breath, but she turned her back to us as if she was giving us privacy.

"I'm not staying here." I didn't mean it, but I was desperate to make him as off-kilter as I felt.

Evren moved slowly around me, and I shifted my body to mirror his. Something Thalia had taught me.

"And where will you go, Adara?" His power shot out and hit my left hand. I hissed and lifted it against my side. He used enough power to make it sting.

I shook out my hand and watched him. "I don't know."

"That's because there is nowhere for you to go." Evren sent out another shot of power, and this time, it hit my other hand.

"Stop it," I demanded of him, but he didn't listen.

"Make me, princess." He cocked his head and studied me. "Show me what Thalia has been training you to do."

I shook my head softly, but he wasn't having it.

"Make me stop." His words were controlled and did nothing but fuel my anger.

I could feel it rising. Irritation over what he was doing, rage over the life we had been dealt.

I was angry, and he was only making it worse. He pushed and pushed and pushed until he gave me no other choice.

I could feel my magic rising inside of me like my anger was a living, palpable thing. I tried to push it down, to control it like Thalia had taught me to, but he was making it impossible.

Another stream of his power shot out, and I slammed my own magic into it before he could hit me. Evren grinned.

"Stop."

But he wasn't listening to me. His black smoke left his fingers once more and his magic came at me so quickly that I wasn't prepared. But I still managed to block it with my own within the last second.

"Good," he encouraged me, and I gritted my teeth as sweat rolled down my back. "Stop trying to see where my power is coming from with your eyes. Feel it in your gut. Trust it."

Anger rose inside of me, and in that moment, I could feel it, his power rising to the left and before I could think better of it, I let my own power slam into the left side of him. It hardly made an impact, his body barely budging, but it was the surprise in his eyes that made me smile.

"Feel it in your gut, Evren. You should have seen that coming."

He smiled then, the look predatory, and part of me wanted to just run inside and hide. I wanted to lock myself in the room and not have to deal with this, but another part of me, a much bigger part, wanted to fight. I wanted to show him what I was capable of.

I wanted to prove to them all that they were underestimating me.

"You're right." He grinned harder. "I should have."

Another stream of his power shot toward me, but I was too busy staring at his handsome face to notice. It hit my right hip, barely knocking into me, and I felt like he was toying with me.

"Is that all you've got?"

"For someone like you, yes?"

"What the hell is that supposed to mean?" I balled my hands into fists as I stared at him and noticed that Thalia had left us completely alone. The traitor.

"You're weak." He nodded toward me, and I bared my teeth. "If you were to leave like you say you want to, you wouldn't survive a day."

"You don't know anything about me," I growled out, and that only made him smile harder.

"Yes. I do." He nodded and moved to his left.

I countered his movements step for step and kept him squarely in front of me.

"I know that you want me even though you don't want to admit it."

I scoffed, but he continued.

"I know that you are capable of so much more than you are allowing yourself." He nodded toward my hands, where my magic was still swirling from my fingertips. "And I know that the sound you make when you come against your own fingers is so much quieter than when you come against mine."

My magic shot out of me before I could control myself, and it slammed directly into Evren's stomach. His breath fell from his lips in a rush just before his ass hit the ground.

I should have felt remorse as I watched him wince, but I couldn't bring myself to do so.

I heard the door open behind me, but Evren simply waved away whoever it was.

"Is someone coming to help the prince from his weak little mate?"

Evren leaned forward and pressed his arms to his knees. "I don't think you're weak, princess. I think you're scared."

He was right. I was scared. I was fearful of letting myself fall into him completely. Holding on to that fear and every ounce of anger I had left was the only way I could protect myself.

"I think you are capable of far more than even you are willing to believe."

I didn't want to listen to him. Not a single word. So I turned on my heel to walk away from him, but his voice stopped me.

"Hit me again."

I looked at him over my shoulder like he was crazy. "No."

"Do it, princess." He ran his hand over his mouth. "Hit me again and this time use every bit of power you can muster."

"I'm not doing it." I shook my head as my hands trembled at my sides.

"Hit me with your power," he growled at me, and my magic bowed and writhed at the sound of his command.

"I don't answer to you, Evren."

He laughed, low and harsh. "You're going to answer to someone, princess, if you don't learn to use your power. Whether it be me or my brother. Is that what you want? To be the Starblessed girl who answered to someone else?"

I balled my hand into a fist as my magic begged me to let it do exactly what he was asking. "And what of you?" I nodded in his direction. "Do you answer to no one or are you simply a pawn in a game of queens?"

His jaw clenched. "Is that what you really think of me, princess?"

"I hardly think of you at all."

His mouth curved up in a wicked smile as he looked up at me. "Gods, you're fucking beautiful, but I think I've told you before that you aren't a very good liar. If you weren't thinking of me, you wouldn't be sleeping in my bed while I was gone." He pushed from the ground and stood back to his full height. I watched as he stared at me. "You wouldn't be pleasuring yourself with your fingers buried between your thighs while I watched, would you?"

When I didn't answer, he continued.

"There are far worse things you could do than think of me, princess."

My hands trembled at my sides.

"And yet, I can't think of anything." I pressed my hands against my hips as I watched him take me in. "What could be worse than a girl thinking about the man who betrayed her?"

His eyes narrowed even though he tried to hide it. "There are many things."

He stepped closer to me, and I held my ground. I didn't want him to see how much he affected me.

"I could never get to touch you again." Another step closer and my mark sparked against my skin. "I could never taste your blood on my lips or feel the power of my mate coursing through me like a fucking drug."

My breath shuddered out of me, but he didn't stop. Another step closer. Then another until he was but a few steps away. "You could refuse my hand even though it's exactly what you want, and you could let my brother take you away from me."

He stepped closer still until the toe of his boots pressed against mine. "There are a million things I can think of that would be worse than my mate thinking of me."

I wanted to retort with something to mess with his head as much as he was mine, but I could barely remember to breathe as he looked down at me and pushed his hand through my hair at the base of my neck. He gripped me there, forcing my head to tilt up to look at him, and my chest heaved with the struggle to remember why I didn't want him.

"But I would much rather think of a million things that I could do to you." His gaze ran over me. "Every moment that I was away, I dreamt of the things I would do to your body. The things that I could teach you." His thumb slowly dragged along my jaw in a lazy pass as he stared down at my mouth. "I dreamt of our wedding night. Of what it will feel like to be inside of you when you are completely mine and mine alone."

I gasped at his words and an ache began between my thighs as my traitorous body reacted to everything he said. Gods, I could imagine it too.

He ran his thumb over the artery in my neck, tracing my racing pulse as he licked his bottom lip. "You can keep telling me that isn't what you want as well, princess, but your body tells differently."

He widened the curve of my neck even further and pressed his nose against the same spot he had just been touching. He inhaled deeply before the soft groan passed his lips. He pressed his mouth against my skin, soft, subtle, a ghost of what I wanted him to do to me, before he spoke again. "When we do wed, there won't be a single part of you that you can hide from me. Everything that you are will belong to me. Just as you possess everything that I am."

His words were so sure, a promise of what was to come, and I shook my head even as I felt the truth of them. "That will never happen."

"How does that lie taste?" I felt him smile against my neck before he gently grazed his teeth against my skin. "I haven't tasted a single part of you that I didn't like." His tongue followed his teeth, and I shuddered beneath him. "If you need to lie to yourself to be okay with what's happening, then do it." He slowly dropped his hand from my skin and took a step back. "I'll take whatever fucking part of you I can get."

He turned from me then and walked away before I could mutter a single word.

FIFTEEN

"Remind me why you insist on my attendance." I stared at Thalia in the mirror where she was still fussing with my hair.

"Because." She grinned as she wrapped a piece of hair around her finger. "Tonight is the Twin Blood Moon Festival. It is the one night of the year when the twin moons will be at their fullest. It is a day of luck and honor, and it symbolizes the prosperity for the year to come." She grabbed a small pot of rouge from her bag that lay on my desk before bringing it to my face. "Evren celebrates with the kingdom every year."

"And what does that have to do with me? Let Evren go out and frolic, and do what he must, but I want to stay here and read." I tapped my finger against the book she had given me, the one about our Starblessed history. Most of what I had read so far was nothing more than things I had already known, but I wasn't even a fourth of the way through. I had just started a section that spoke of Starblessed amplifying their magic with nature.

I was far more interested in it than standing before Evren and falling for his every word.

Because that was what I had been doing. I hadn't seen him

since yesterday in the courtyard, and his damned words replayed over and over in my head.

"You have plenty of time to read later. I suppose you could stay in and attend the queen's annual dinner." I scrunched my nose, and she laughed as she pressed some rouge against my cheeks before picking up a pot of red cream and dipping her finger inside. She slid it across my lips, and I held perfectly still as she did so. "I'm certain you'll enjoy tonight's festivities."

She moved out of the way, and I stared at myself in the mirror. She had lined my eyes with coal and my lips were a sharp contrast that matched the color of blood. The same color as the dress she had brought that hung near my bed.

"You'll stay with me the whole time?" I stood and moved toward the dress. I lifted the light skirt in my hands and looked upon it. It was much finer than anything I had ever worn back home, finer than anything I had ever worn until I arrived at Gavril's side.

A chill ran over my skin, and I tried not to allow myself to think of him. My gaze fell to my wrist, but I quickly pulled it away to look at my friend.

She was dressed similarly, with her dark, curly hair framing her face beautifully, and her dress fell behind her in the lightest shade of blue.

It was odd to watch how graceful she seemed in the gown because I had never seen her in anything other than trousers and a shirt.

"Yes." She chuckled at my question. "I promise I won't leave you alone so you aren't tempted to sneak off into the dark with your mate."

I swatted her arm, but she chuckled harder.

"That is not going to happen." I slipped my shirt over my head as she pulled my dress from where it hung and held it out to me. I stepped inside, the silky fabric gliding against my skin, and I turned away from her as she began to lace up the bodice.

"You're right. It'll probably be the other way around. Evren's going to want to tear this dress off you as soon as he sees you."

I scoffed at her before moving to the mirror and fussing with the small earrings she had given me. I stared at my reflection, and I hardly recognized the girl looking back at me.

The red dress dipped low between my breasts and the sheer sleeves covered my arms all the way down to my wrists. The slit in the gown came up to my hip and left my left leg on full display.

But it was the back that had me doing a double take. It was so unlike anything I had ever worn in the fae kingdom because the star marks on my back were completely covered by the fabric.

This wasn't a dress to display me as a Starblessed. If anything, it displayed me as Evren's mate.

It was odd. I looked so unlike myself, but at the same time, I felt more me than I ever had before. Stronger. More sure. I had no idea how I could feel that way when I felt so confused at the same time. It was as if I was discovering who I was, but still so unsure about who I wanted to be.

But even that was a lie.

I wanted to be Evren's mate. I wanted to tell him yes when he joked about taking his hand, but there was another part of me that was still so fearful. Even though I had felt more at home in the Blood kingdom than I had ever felt anywhere else, I was scared to let that feeling be real.

I looked in the mirror, and I watched Thalia as she fussed with the strap of her shoe around her ankle. For the first time in my life, I felt like I had found home in a friend, and that almost made me more fearful than Evren did.

Thalia had become my best friend, and I feared the heart break of losing her.

"Okay. Come on." Thalia headed in my direction and

grabbed my hand in hers. She pulled me toward the door as a smile lit up her face. "We're going to miss all the fun."

I smiled and tried to push down my intrusive thoughts because her joy was contagious.

She pulled me along with her, not stopping until we pushed outside the castle doors. I took a deep breath as I stared up into the sky and saw the twin moons shining at their fullest. Back home this day had been a bad omen. It was a day when stories were told of the vampyres and what they were capable of. It was a day when we were warned of the dangers that lurked just outside the edge of our town.

But I felt none of that fear here.

Instead, people were bustling around the palace and through the streets. Flowers were tied together and hung from posts and through the trees. A small boy ran past me, his laughter filling the air.

"This way." Thalia nodded forward, and I followed her through the small courtyard at the front of the castle and toward the streets.

More laughter rang out as my feet hit the cobblestone, and Thalia stopped at the closest vendor and handed him a coin. The man handed her two small bunches of wildflowers, and she passed one to me before thanking him.

"It's customary." She held up the flowers as we walked. "To lay a flower on the doorstep of anyone you wish prosperity for the year." She dropped a flower at the first shop we passed. "Evren drops a flower on every doorstep in the kingdom."

My chest ached and I wanted to roll my eyes at how damn endearing she made him sound. "Are you trying to make me like him?" We passed another door, and this time, I stopped and laid one of my flowers on the stoop.

"You already like him." She shook her head as she rolled her eyes. "I'm just trying to prove to you that there is nothing wrong with that fact."

"Maybe I don't like him at all. Maybe I just find him insanely attractive."

"Who's insanely attractive?" Evren asked, and I almost dropped all of my flowers as I spun to face him.

"Sorin." The name fell from my lips, and Sorin grinned next to him.

"The feeling is mutual, Adara. I've already told you what would happen if you weren't Evren's mate." His smile dropped from his lips as Evren's hand slammed across his chest. "Shit. I was just joking around."

But Evren was no longer looking at him. He was too busy staring at me.

"Princess, you look…" He shook his head softly as if he couldn't complete his sentence.

"What?" I asked softly, and he took a step closer to me, closing the space between us.

He wore his normal black, but his clothes were freshly pressed and molded to his skin. He wore a small pin against his chest. A dagger with a serpent coiling around it almost protectively.

He stepped even closer, and I pulled my gaze away from the pin to look up at him.

"You look absolutely stunning, princess." He lifted his hand and ran his finger over my hair that fell against my shoulder. "Like a fucking dream."

My marks stirred along with my magic, and I tried to swallow down the emotion that flooded me with his words. "What's this?" I ran my finger along his pin, and my magic quivered at the contact.

"That's the crest of the Blood kingdom. The crest of my mother." His voice was soft as he spoke to me.

"I don't trust your mother."

He chuckled and his hand trailed over my shoulder. "I would find you foolish if you did so blindly."

"Yet you do?"

"I am much like my mother." He looked to the side when someone called his name and nodded in their direction. "Every decision she makes is one for her people."

"She sent her men to attack you." My blood boiled as I said it, and I knew that regardless of why she made the decisions she did, I would never forgive her for that.

"She sent her men to save you."

I shook my head, and Evren took my hand in his. I smiled at a few people that were passing by, and each of them looked so in awe of their prince.

"Come on." He pulled me after him, and even though I tried to pull my hand from his, he refused to let go.

Sorin and Thalia were just ahead of us, and Thalia was still laying flowers upon every doorstep she walked by. I watched the people of Evren's kingdom as we passed. Each one of them was dressed in their best, and they nodded or bowed their heads in Evren's direction as we passed.

"Your people really love you."

He looked back at me, and an odd look passed over his face. "I'm not too sure of that, but I try to always treat them with respect and honor."

I cocked my head and studied him. "You're so different."

"What do you mean?" He chuckled and his hand tightened against mine.

"Prince Evren." I waved my other hand toward him just as he said a soft hello to an older woman as we passed. "And the Evren that I know. They are two completely different people."

Evren stopped and tugged my hand forward until I had no choice but to slam into his chest.

"What are you…"

He lifted his other hand and ran his thumb just below my bottom lip. "I can't see this color on your lips and not imagine what they would look like wrapped around my cock."

"Evren!" I hissed his name and looked around to make sure no one else could hear him.

"The prince you see with his kingdom and the one you know are the same." His thumb moved softly against my skin, and my mouth fell open as I watched him. "You can't fathom the amount of control it takes for me to stand here and wish people a Happy Twin Blood Moon when all I really want to do is rip this fucking dress from your skin and worship every damn inch of you."

I gasped and started to pull away, but his fist hooked under my chin.

"You cannot comprehend the agony I feel to watch my mate and not have a clue as to what's going through that beautiful head of yours."

"You." The word passed my lips before I could stop them.

"Princess," he growled just as Thalia and Sorin joined us.

"They've got a game of silvers going on at The Olde Vine. Come on. Adara and I against you two." Thalia rubbed her hands together, and I pulled my face away from Evren's grip.

"I don't know what silvers is."

"Even better." Sorin laughed. "That means that Evren and I are definitely going to win."

I lifted my dress in my hand and followed them toward the small pub. Evren smiled as he motioned me forward, and I could hardly control the flutter in my stomach.

The Olde Vine looked so different from the last time we were here. Candles were scattered over the bar and throughout the tables. Little flowers hung from the ceiling and scattered across the floor.

"Here you go." Evren pulled a silver coin from his pocket and held it out to me.

"What am I supposed to do with this?" I flipped it over in my fingers.

Evren moved around me and pressed his chest to my back. "That glass right there." He pointed to the mug in the middle of the table. "You have to bounce your silver at least once before you hit it into the mug."

"If I get it in the mug, I win?"

"If you get it in, you get a point." He chuckled softly.

"And if I miss?"

"If you miss… you owe me a kiss," he whispered against my shoulder.

"That isn't true."

"I don't make the rules, princess." He moved around me and stood at my side. "I just follow them."

"Sorin is on your team too. I could simply kiss him for every time I miss."

There was a flash in Evren's eyes, and his teeth clenched together as a low growl escaped. "If you'd like to see me kill my best friend and captain, sure." His hand trailed over mine, his fingers casually touching my own. "But I think Sorin has his hands full with Thalia."

I looked across the table, and he was right. The two of them were arguing about something, and I couldn't stop my small snort of laughter.

"Where's Jorah?"

"You just looking for anyone else to kiss besides me?" He grinned, but it didn't fully meet his eyes.

"That's not what I meant." I had been so relieved that Evren was home, so confused, that I hadn't even thought of anything else. Anyone else.

Evren nodded once as if he understood. "He and a few of my men are closely watching the border. He should be back in a couple days."

"So how does this friendship work exactly." I waved my hand toward Sorin as I slid the piece of silver from one hand to the other.

"Sorin has been my best friend since we were children." Evren nodded in his direction. "He is the captain of my army and my most trusted. He would give his life for me, and I would do the same."

"And Jorah?"

"Jorah came into my life a lot later than Sorin, but he has stood at my side since I met him. The three of us have been inseparable for many years."

"Why did you take Jorah with you to the fae kingdom instead of Sorin?"

"Because I needed him here." His gaze slid to Sorin where he was tucking one of Thalia's curls behind her ear. She quickly swatted his hand away. "I knew that if something happened to me, if I didn't return, that Sorin's hands were the ones I would want my kingdom to fall into."

"But your mother?"

"My mother rules because she was born to do so. Not because of her want. Our kingdom loves her, but she would rather live in a small home in the hills and never have to be in the palace again."

My heart raced at his words because they were the last thing I expected. I thought Queen Veda to be ruthless and cunning. But what he was saying was the opposite.

"I don't understand." I shook my head.

He leaned in closer and pressed his mouth to my ear. "Let's talk about this later. I'm eager to watch you lose."

I could feel a blush creeping up my chest. "And what if you lose?"

"Then I'll owe you a kiss for each one I miss." He lifted his hand and gently wrapped it around the back of my neck. "And you'll get to choose exactly where I pay my price. Here." He ran his finger over the side of my neck. "Or here." He lifted his other hand and ran his thumb along my bottom lip. "Or I can bury myself between your thighs and pay my price with my tongue."

"Are you two ready?"

My gaze slammed into Thalia's, and I knew that I had to be as red as the flowers that hung around the bar.

"We're ready." Evren didn't miss a beat, and I knew this was exactly what he wanted. To throw me completely off guard, to make me think of nothing but my want for him.

"Ladies first." He nodded in my direction, and my fingers shook around my piece of silver as I stepped up to the table. I stared at the mug in the middle of the large wooden table and took a deep breath. Evren was still at my back, still a force I couldn't ignore, and he was all I could think about as I let the silver slip through my fingers and bounce against the table. It hit once, then twice before careening in the direction of the mug. On the last hop, it hit the rim of the mug before slowly falling down against the table.

"Oh my gods. That was so close." Thalia clapped her hands, and Evren simply grinned at me.

"My turn." Evren grabbed his silver coin and moved in front of me to line himself up. He hardly thought of the task before he launched the coin down the table. It bounced once before it landed perfectly in the mug, and he turned back toward me with a wide grin on his face. I couldn't stop myself from returning it.

"Lucky shot, prince." I crossed my arms as Thalia grabbed her coin and launched it toward the mug just as Evren moved around me.

"Did I forget to mention that I was skilled at this?" He chuckled as he faced me. "Sorin and I used to play this game as often as we could to get away from our studies."

"So you made me place a bad bet already knowing the outcome." I cocked an eyebrow at him. "That's not very princely of you."

"I never said I played fair, princess. Especially not when it comes to you." Thalia's coin landed in the mug, but I couldn't concentrate on anything other than him. "I'll play as dirty as a need to."

Sorin threw his coin, and it barely made it in. Sorin rubbed his hand along the back of his neck as he released a deep breath, and Thalia laughed.

Evren held another coin in my direction. "Your turn, princess." He was staring at my mouth, and I couldn't bring myself to care about the stupid game. I couldn't think of anything other than the way he was looking at me, and what it would feel like to have his fingers pull this dress from my skin.

"Stop trying to distract my teammate." Thalia slammed her hands down on the table. "Do not make me separate you two."

Evren held his hands up in defense as he laughed. "I'm not doing anything." He smiled at Thalia, his charm in full force, but she simply rolled her eyes.

Before he could turn back to look at me, I focused on the mug and tossed the coin on the table with more force than last time. It hit the table once with a loud thud before bouncing and landing straight in the mug.

Thalia's mouth dropped open, and I squealed so loudly I was sure that I scared some of the patrons. But it didn't matter, Thalia came toward me, and the two of us slapped hands in celebration.

I turned back to Evren, and he was watching me with a smile on his handsome face.

I held up a finger. "So far, you only get one." He laughed and looked toward the mug. "The game is still young, princess. The first team to make it to ten wins."

I cross my arms and grinned to him. "And right now, we're tied."

He moved closer to me even though it was his turn to go. "Would you like to sweeten the bet?" he whispered against my ear.

"How so?" I swallowed deeply as the smell of him over-whelmed me.

"If I win, I get your hand, and you take my last name." My gaze slammed into his, but he was being serious. He was saying it so calmly as if we weren't betting our future on a game of silvers.

"And if I win?"

"Whatever you want. If you win, I promise to give you whatever it is you want."

"Even my freedom?"

His throat moved as he swallowed hard, and his gaze searched mine. I expected him to take it back, to tell me we weren't going to do this on a game, but he surprised me once again.

"If that's what you choose." He nodded. "You don't have to decide now, but I'll give you whatever it is you choose." He held out his hand, and I stared at it. "Do we have a deal?"

I slid my hand into his before I could talk myself out of it, and his tightened around mine.

"Deal." I felt his magic zap through me. Not just his, ours. Our magic combined, solidifying the wager I had just placed, and Evren's gaze darkened as if he found pleasure in my magic touching his.

"All right, princess. Let's play." He took his silver coin and threw it against the table. It bounced once before once again landing perfectly in his mug, and I cursed under my breath.

Thalia shot a look in my direction before her gaze slid to Evren. Did she know? Was she more than aware of how foolish I was when it came to her prince?

Evren barely paid me a bit of attention for the rest of the game, his focus solely on winning, and mine was on my anxiety as I watched Sorin flip his coin in the air. The score was nine to eight, and I had been the only one to miss my shot the entire game.

"It was fun playing with you ladies." Sorin laughed before catching his coin back in his hand. "But you all should practice before going up against us again."

"Just go." Thalia crossed her arms, and Sorin chuckled

before launching the coin toward the mug. It bounced once, twice, a third time before making its way toward the mug. My magic flared inside of me as if it knew the deal I had just made. The foolish, reckless deal.

I stared at the mug and the only thing that could run through my mind was *please don't make it.*

The coin hit the lip of the mug before slowly rolling across the edge, and I felt like everyone in the entire pub was silent as we watched it. It rolled and rolled until it paused, standing on the edge with perfect balance, before slowly falling over and landing on the table.

Silence rang out through the pub before Sorin destroyed it.

"That's shit!" He looked between the three of us. "Which one of you used your magic to make sure I didn't make it?"

Thalia laughed. "You can't just admit that sometimes you aren't very good at things?"

Sorin's gaze swung in my direction, and I held up my hands. "You saw me training with Thalia. I do not have that kind of control of my magic."

I felt a hand caress down my spine, my mark sparking to life, and I turned in Evren's direction. But he wasn't touching me, it was his magic.

"We haven't lost yet." Evren ran his hand over his jaw. "Let Adara have her turn."

His gaze slid toward mine, and I could see it hiding there. The lie he had just told. It was his magic that stopped that coin. It was his magic that took away their win and refused to take away my choice.

I watched him as he smiled at me softly, and he was so unlike his brother in that moment. His brother who would take anything from me that he had deemed his own.

But Evren didn't want that.

Evren wanted me to choose him because I wanted to. Of

course, I was a part of the plan to save his kingdom, but this was more than that.

I guess we had been since the moment we met.

I lined myself back up with shaking hands as I grasped the coin. I had no idea what I was doing. No idea what I wanted, but I still lifted the coin and threw it toward the mug.

It hit the table and bounced four times before making its way toward the mug. I held my breath as I watched it land on the other coins that the mug held.

"We're tied." Evren smiled and rolled his coin through his fingers. "Which means this is for the winning point."

"It is." I pressed my hands against the table and leaned back against it. "If you make it, you win. If you don't, then our fate will be in Thalia's hands."

"It seems that's the way our fate always goes, isn't it? Left in the hands of others." He ran his hand over his jaw as he stared down at my mouth.

"I hate that. Don't you?" I cocked my head and studied him.

"Despise it."

"Yet we do nothing to change it." I crossed my arms, and Evren's gaze fell to my breasts.

"Haven't we?" He leaned forward and pressed a hand to the table on either side of me. He leaned forward, his mouth close to mine. "You are here with me instead of with my brother which fate promised you."

"I was never meant for your brother," I answered, and Evren's breath rushed out of him. "A promise between mothers is not fate."

"No." He shook his head. "It's not."

Evren stared at me for a few long moments, and his gaze fluttering over my face until it lingered on my lips. For a moment, I thought that he would push forward and kiss me. Right here in front of all these people, but he seemed to catch himself at the last moment before he pulled away and stood to his full height.

He held the coin between his fingers, and he stared down at it before looking toward the mug. He hadn't missed a single shot all night, and I knew that he wouldn't miss this one. His coin would land in that glass mug, and my fate would be sealed even more so than it already was. My fate would laugh at me for making such a foolish deal, a deal I couldn't back out of.

Evren lifted his arm, ready to throw, and I still hadn't moved from my spot at the table. I watched him as he looked over at me, and there was so much hesitation in his eyes. So much doubt. And he didn't take his eyes off me as he flung the coin from his hand, not once looking to the table. I didn't turn around to look, I didn't need to. I just stared ahead at my mate and my soon-to-be husband.

"Oh my gods!" Thalia's voice rang out, and I pulled my gaze away from Evren to look behind me. To look at his coin that had missed the mug and laid on the other side of it.

I swung my gaze back to meet his. "You missed." I wasn't sure if it was a question or an accusation, either way, a small grin graced his lips.

"Even princes make mistakes." He shrugged simply. "I didn't have it in me to take away your fate. So, let's leave it up to someone else."

I stared at him as I tried to catch my breath. As I tried to think about what he had just done. He could've easily won just now and had everything he had been asking for, but he chose not to.

It was his fate as much as it was mine, and he still chose not to. It was on the tip of my tongue to tell Thalia to miss. To tell her to let them win so I had no choice but to make good on the deal I had given him, but I couldn't force myself to say it. Not before she grabbed the coin in her hand and launched it toward the mug. It bounced twice before clinging against the glass, and I heard her scream of victory ring out through the pub.

Everyone around us cheered and celebrated, and Evren grinned at me as if he was happy that we had won, but I couldn't stop the sinking feeling in my gut. Was I not happy that we won?

"Well, it appears that you won." Evren moved closer to me and lifted my hand in his. "But it wasn't a total loss. You still owe me that kiss."

"And you owe me one as well."

"True." He pushed forward until his thighs pressed against my knees. "Should I lay you back on this table and give you your prize now?" His hands dropped to my thighs and pressed against the fabric of my dress.

My breath caught in my throat as I thought about what he was saying. As I thought about how badly I wished the rest of this pub would just disappear so he could do exactly what he was telling me.

"Here." Thalia shoved a glass of wine in my hand, and she couldn't hide the grin on her face. "Whatever you did to mess Evren up, I am forever grateful in your debt. I have never been able to beat these two."

I shook my head gently. "I didn't do anything."

"Don't let her lie to you, Thalia. She did far more than even she realizes."

Thalia looked back and forth between us, and there was a spark of mischief in her eyes as she watched us. "Come on. The moons will be at their fullest in a few minutes. We should get outside."

Evren grabbed my hand and helped me down from the table, and he didn't drop it even as we walked out of the pub. Sorin led the way with a defeated pout on his face, and I couldn't help but laugh.

"Go ahead, Adara." Sorin shot me a look. "You might as well

celebrate because this will be the one and only time you all beat us."

I laughed again as we pushed through the crowd, the streets had gotten busier since we entered the pub. Everyone was taking to the streets to watch the moons, and their prince stood amongst them.

He didn't move to push his way to the front or demand an audience to notice he was there. He simply stood with his people and looked to the sky as he searched for the moons that promised prosperity.

He moved me in front of him and pressed his chest against my back. "Any moment now." He wrapped his arms around me and held me against him.

I could feel people watching us, dissecting our every move, but I couldn't bring myself to push him away.

"The twin blood moons are considered a bad omen in the human lands," I whispered the tale I had been told for many years to distract myself from the way my hands trembled before me.

Evren scoffed and pushed a bit of my hair over my shoulder. "And what exactly do they think happens with the blood moons?"

"Vampyres." I smiled up at him over my shoulder. "It is legend that any human that isn't locked away in safety during the twin blood moons would be taken by a vampyre who is being driven mad with thirst."

Evren chuckled as if the thought was ridiculous. "So what? You all bar up your doors and spread your salt in an effort to keep us away?" A chill ran down my spine as I simply nodded my head.

"That's exactly what we do." I stared up at his jaw as he searched the sky. "But I'm assuming neither would actually keep you away if you wanted in."

He looked back down at me, and his eyes seemed darker than

only a moment before. "Princess, there isn't a single thing in this world or the next that could keep me away from you."

I let out a breath as my magic flared inside of me and my heart raced to an erratic beat.

"There." Evren pointed to the sky, and I pulled my attention away from him for long enough to look up at the moons. Both were perfect circles, still mostly the cream color that normally hearkened our skies, but ever so slowly the tent of blood pushed along the bottom surface.

"In the Blood Court, the double blood moons is our season of change," Evren spoke softly against my ear as he still stared up at the sky. "They are a sign of what is to come. But the moons don't determine our future, princess. It is up to us to make something of the prosperity they give us."

The vampyres that surrounded us were gasping and taking in the moons. Some held their hands up toward the sky, while others simply took it in with wishful eyes.

"I want to show you something," Evren whispered against my ear, and a tremor ran down my spine.

"Okay." I nodded as he took my hand in his and pulled me toward him. He led me through the crowd, and almost none of them paid us any attention as we got lost among them.

He pulled me through the crowd, and I didn't question where we were going. I simply held my hand in his and let him pull me to wherever he wanted me to go.

We broke through the line of people, and I lifted the hem of my dress with my other hand as we moved down one of the side cobblestone streets. Evren looked back at me with a smile on his face, and my stomach fluttered as I watched his joy.

"Just a little bit farther." He continued forward until we slid around the back of the building and into the grass.

"Hold on." I pulled my hand from his and quickly pulled my shoes from my feet. My toes sunk into the cold grass, and I let my shoes dangle from my fingers as I gathered my dress once again.

Evren swallowed as he watched me, and he backed out toward the line of trees.

"Are you luring me to my death?" I laughed even as my stomach flipped. "Maybe the legends of the human lands aren't as far-fetched as you had me believe."

Evren chuckled as he ran his hand down his chest. "I may be luring you away, princess. But it isn't for your death. I could've done that long ago if that was what I wanted from you."

"You think so little of me?"

"The contrary, princess. I think far more of you than I ever have anyone else." He reached his hand out toward me, and I slid mine back into his as he pulled us out of the light of the moons and into the shadows of the trees.

"Then what exactly are you luring me into the forest for?"

He didn't answer me at first. He simply pulled me deeper into the dense trees as I tried to match him step for step. The trees were thick with moss that hung from their branches and kissed against my cheeks.

He pushed some out of the way as a small clearing came into view. "This."

I moved past him until I could finally see what he was showing me. A small creek flowed through the trees, almost hidden beyond the rocks and moss that clung to their surface.

"This is beautiful." I looked around before glancing back over my shoulder toward the town. "I would have never known this was here."

"It's one of my favorite places in the kingdom." He leaned against a rock and kicked off his boots. "I come here often when I need to clear my head."

He tossed his boots to the side before he pulled a small dagger from his side that I hadn't even noticed. He laid it against his boots then started pulling the tail of his shirt from his pants.

"What are you doing?" I clung to my dress even though I couldn't stop looking at him.

"This isn't what I wanted to show you." He pulled his shirt over his head and dropped it on the ground. I stared at the way the moonlight reflected against his skin, and my gaze caught on the newest scar that marred him. "We've got to wade through the creek to get to it."

I lifted the skirt of my dress before looking at him like he was crazy. "I'm in a gown."

"A beautiful fucking gown at that. One that has made me think of nothing but ripping it off you since the moment I saw you tonight." His gaze ran over the length of me, and it felt like a caress. "I suggest you take it off easily unless you'd like me to do just that."

I wrapped my arms around myself as he unbuttoned his trousers and started pulling them from his hips. He didn't take his gaze off me, and all I could think about were the red lacy undergarments that Thalia had convinced me to wear under the dress. There was no way in hell I could pull this dress from my skin and let him see it.

"Take it off." Evren nodded toward me as he kicked his trousers off his legs. He was left in nothing but a pair of white undergarments, and I took a small step back. "Princess, I wasn't kidding. I will rip that dress off you. Don't try to hide what's beneath. I've seen every inch of your body, pressed my fingers against it, worshipped it with my tongue. "

He took a step in my direction, and I held out my hands. "Okay." I reached behind me and slowly undid the laces of my dress with trembling fingers. I slid my arms out of the sleeves and held the bodice against my chest as I watched him watch me. It was just me and him and the twin blood moons, but somehow, I felt more exposed than ever. I took a deep breath before letting my dress pool at my feet.

"Fuck." He ran his hand over his jaw as his gaze hungrily took me in. "This is probably a bad idea."

"What?" I scrambled to grab my dress, but his hands quickly stopped me.

"Don't even think about putting that dress back on." His voice was firm and wild.

"You're the one who just said this is a bad idea."

"That's because I didn't realize that you would look like that beneath." He motioned toward my body. "I had planned on showing some restraint with my mate tonight." He bit down on his bottom lip. "Now the only thought running through my head is how I'm going to devour every inch of you."

"Evren." My voice shook along with my hands as he pulled me toward him.

"Come on. If I don't show you now, we'll never make it there."

I let him pull me into the brook and the warm water lapped at my ankles. Evren chuckled as I almost slipped on a rock, and I slapped his chest just as he wrapped an arm around my middle.

"The water isn't but a few inches deep here. It would be embarrassing for the legends of the kingdom's prince and princess to have found their demise in the small brook behind the town."

I laughed even as the butterflies took off in my stomach. "But I'm not their princess."

"Not yet." He kept walking, moving us forward, and I had to admit that the water felt good against my legs even as we inched deeper and deeper.

We were headed to the other side of the brook where boulders laid upon one another all covered in moss and trails of water. I had no idea where he was taking me. But I still allowed him to move me forward with his body against mine.

"Almost there." He led me a few steps farther until my hand touched the boulder in front of us.

"You're right. This boulder is a sight to behold."

Evren chuckled and pulled me to the right. He didn't say a word as he pushed around the boulder, and I noticed the smallest slit between two of the rocks. My heart hammered in my chest as he squeezed between them, but he didn't let go of my hand. He pulled me after him, and I followed his steps as I pushed between the rocks until I could no longer see the light of the moons.

"I'm not sure about this," I whispered as I pushed out from between the rocks, and the water lapping at my hips.

"Just a little farther." Evren's hand hadn't left mine, and he continued to pull me through the rocks. They pushed against my stomach and chest, almost too tight to squeeze through, and I took a sharp breath once I finally cleared them and hit Evren's chest. "This is what I wanted to show you."

I looked around the dark cave and gasped at the starlight that covered every surface of the ceiling. I had never seen starlight except what marked my skin. It was legend that the stars had burned out over a hundred years ago.

"How?" I moved deeper into the cave, and Evren stayed with me step for step with his chest pressed against my back.

"They're called glowworms." Evren pointed over my shoulder to where a strong cluster of light shined from the ceiling. "I don't know much about them, but they've always been here since I first discovered this place as a child."

"They look like stars." I lifted my hand toward one, but I was far too short to reach them.

"They remind me of them, yes." He moved around me and let his fingers trail through the water. "This place reminds me of you."

"I thought you spent most of your childhood in the fae kingdom."

"I did once I was taken from my mother." He nodded and

looked around the cave. "But I spent the first ten years of my life here."

"And your father didn't know about you."

"I think he always thought he could keep me hidden."

"What changed?"

"Queen Kaida learned of the prophecy and decided she would no longer leave fate up to chance." He looked back toward me. "So my father went to war with my kingdom to take me back with him."

"And he won."

"My mother didn't stand a chance of fighting him off. She was unprepared and too busy being a mother to let the threats of other kingdoms cloud her mind. She had let a man who she thought she once loved become harmless in her mind. It cost her dearly."

"She lost you."

"And her father." Evren moved in front of me and his knees bumped against mine. "My father took both of us from her on the same day. She lost her child and became a queen. Neither of which she was ready for."

My chest ached as I thought about the pain she must have felt that day. I couldn't fathom the pain he must have endured.

"I'm sorry."

"Don't be." He shook his head and lifted his wet hand to push some hair out of my face. "It was a long time ago."

"I'm still sorry just the same."

"You're sorry for a man you hate?" His hand pressed against my jaw and lifted it until I was forced to look at him.

"I don't hate you."

"You should." His fingers caressed my jaw and water trailed from them and down my neck. "It is selfish of me to wish that you don't."

"Because you need me to fulfill the prophecy?"

"Because I need you to breathe."

"Evren." His name was a plea on my lips, but he didn't answer me with words. Instead, he closed the space between us and pressed his mouth against mine. There was nothing soft or subtle about it. It was pure longing, and I felt absolutely desperate for him.

I wrapped my arms around his shoulders, pulling me closer to him, and his hands moved to my thighs and gripped them to lift me. I moved my legs around him, my ankles crossing against his back as his fingers dug into my skin.

His hands were as rushed and harsh as his mouth, and I felt bruised. Bruised from his words that affected me far more than I should've allowed them to. Bruised from his kiss that dug into my soul. He was my mate, and every part of me knew it in that moment. He was my mate, and I wanted nothing more.

"I'm infatuated with you," Evren breathed the words against my lips. "Every fucking part of you drives me mad with want."

"Have me." The words rushed out of me as my heart hammered in my chest. "If you want me, have me."

Evren wasted no time. His mouth moved along my jaw before moving down my neck. He lapped at my skin with his tongue before grazing it with his teeth, and pure, unfiltered want raged through me as I tightened my legs around him.

I wanted him more than I had ever wanted anything else before. I wanted to know every detail of his body and every moment that weighed heavy on his mind. I wanted to take that from him, to give him something that only I could, and as I ground down my hips against him, that was all I could think of.

He was mine and I was his, and nothing else could matter in that moment.

Evren's fingers dug in the top of my bra, and he jerked it down my skin before his mouth followed its path. There was nothing gentle about him, every move of his mouth was punishing, and I was desperate for more. I wanted him to mark every inch of me to prove that this was real.

He sucked my nipple into his mouth and looked up at me as I ran my fingers through his dark hair.

His gaze held no hesitancy. He wasn't asking for permission or trying to determine what I wanted. This was him taking. He was taking exactly what he wanted, and I had never wanted anything so much in my life. I leaned into his mouth, as his teeth scraped against my nipple, and I cried out his name.

"Gods, you're so perfect." He peppered more kisses across my chest before he lifted me higher in the water. "I could do nothing but taste every inch of you for hours."

I whimpered as he pressed his tongue over the fabric of my other cup and the pressure felt immensely different on my nipple.

"Evren, please." I begged him as my fingers tugged harder in his hair.

"Tell me what you want, princess. Tell me, and I'll give you anything."

"Make love to me," I said as I continued to grind against him. "I need you to fuck me."

Evren groaned before cursing under his breath, and his hands tightened against me. He moved in the water, taking us farther into the cave, and I could do nothing but hold on to him and grind my body against him in desperation.

He lifted me and turned me until my chest pressed against the cold boulder. His fingers trailed down my spine and left chill bumps in their wake.

His hand moved around my waist, slowly tracing over every inch of skin he could find before they trailed over my hip bone and pressed against the lace of my undergarments.

"I have never wanted anyone more than I want you," he whispered against the back of my neck. "Never thought of anyone, went crazy over anyone, you're all I can see."

His fingers pushed into my undergarments, and he groaned when they met my sex.

His fingers slid over my nub, and I hissed out a breath as

pleasure coursed through me. He pressed his lips to my shoulder and laid a soft kiss there as his fingers pushed harder against me.

"Does anyone else know about this cave?" I tried to look behind me, but he had my body pinned with his.

"It doesn't matter." His teeth grazed against my shoulder. "The entire Blood army could squeeze through those rocks, and they wouldn't be able to stop me from having you."

His hand slid lower until he pushed a finger inside of me, and I held on to the rock in front of me as my knees trembled.

"You're so fucking tight like this." He groaned against my neck. "Just imagine if this was my cock. Imagine how full you're going to feel with me inside of you."

My stomach was tight and my heart was racing, and all I could think about was wanting more. No matter what Evren gave me, it would never be enough. I always wanted more from him.

He slowly pumped his hand in and out of me while his palm pressed firmly against my aching nub. His other hand moved up my body slowly, until he wrapped his fingers around my neck and pulled me back into him. I gasped as he turned my face to meet his and nibbled on my bottom lip.

His hand moved faster and faster, and pleasure raced through me along with something else. Something more that was digging its claws into my chest and refusing to let go.

My magic writhed inside of me, begging for his touch, and I couldn't stop the next words that were falling from my lips, "I hated you for leaving." I breathed against his mouth, and his breath rushed out against me. "I was so damn scared when Jorah's report came back that Queen Kaida knew of your treason. I was so damn scared that you would never return."

"I know." He nodded against me, and my chest shook with every emotion that flowed through me. Evren pressed his nose against my skin and took a deep breath. "Trust me, princess. The thought of never coming back to you ate away at me. I have never been so fearful of my duty before."

I whimpered as his hand continued to move against me, and he grazed his teeth against my shoulder.

"Why did you lose the game?" His hand was driving me crazy, and I could barely think, but I needed to know. I need to know what was going through his head.

"You know why I lost. I don't want to be the man that you think I am. I don't want to be anything like my brother." His palm pressed harder against me and slowed down in speed as he pumped his fingers in harder and harder. "If you stay here, princess. If you decide to take my hand, I want you to do it with your own free will. Not because someone else promised you away or because I won a stupid fucking bet. I want you to *want* to stay here with me."

I reached behind me, gripping my fingers into the hair on the back of his neck, and I held on to him as I started to fall apart. My body trembled from the work of his hands and the truth of his words. His truth both settled me and put me further on edge.

But it was his actions that scared me the most. They showed me that he was the man I thought he was before his duty forced him to betray me. He had chosen the duty to his kingdom over his mate, or at least I thought he had, but the reality was that I was far safer in Evren's hands. I was exactly where I wanted to be even though he had taken that choice away from me.

Now he was giving it back.

"Evren," I called out his name as my body tightened against him. I was so close to the edge, so close to falling, and I felt like I was always on this precipice with him. Just the smallest push would throw me over the edge, but I was always so scared to fall.

"Let go," Evren murmured against my neck where he ran his tongue over my pulse point. "Be a good girl and let go."

As soon as the words fell from his lips, I had no choice but to give him exactly what he wanted. My thighs clamped down around his hand as my body trembled, and I cried out as my pleasure rushed through me and mixed with my magic.

"That's it." Evren's hand moved slowly against me, coaxing out every ounce of pleasure my body had to give. "Give me exactly what's mine."

He continued to kiss me. His mouth running over every inch of my skin, down my back and over my star marks, all while I came down from the pleasure that was soaring through me.

I pushed off the rock and turned toward him. I wrapped my arms around his neck before his mouth met my own. I kissed him hard, desperately, and I didn't know what I was searching for, but my chest ached as his hands gripped my skin and searched over me. He kissed me back with just as much desperation, and the pleasure he had just given me did nothing to take the edge off my want for him.

I wanted him more.

He pulled away from me slightly before running his fingers across my face and pushing my hair out of my eyes. "We should get back to the festival."

My heart dropped and I stared him. "What?"

He wrapped his hand around the back of my neck and stared into my eyes. "This is your first Twin Blood Moon Festival, and you shouldn't spend it hidden away in a cave with me the whole night. "

My fingers dug harder into his flesh, and I couldn't explain it. I didn't want to let him go. I didn't want to leave this cave and face the world around us.

"I want more."

Evren searched my face, and I could see the indecision in his eyes. Whether to stay with me or to go back out there with his people, and I felt pure guilt for making him choose.

"I will give you anything you ever want, princess." He pulled me tighter to him, his arms wrapping around my back and eliminating any space between us. "I don't want to only take pleasure from your body." He searched my face as he said the words "I want all of you. Every moment, every breath. I want to know your heartbreaks and make sure they never happen again. I want to give you every part of me and to take every part of you in return."

My hands trembled against him as my heart raced with his words. It was what I wanted too, and I would've given him that. I would've given him all of that and more if things had been different, but I wasn't sure that I was cut out to be the person he wanted me to be.

He was half fae and half vampyre. He was the son of two nobles who held more power than I could even fathom, and he was choosing me.

"I… Evren, I…"

He ran his hands over my neck as he smiled. "Come on, princess. Let's go get some wine and rejoin the festival."

He moved to pull me from the cave, and I couldn't stop the dread that filled me.

SIXTEEN

I could hardly concentrate as Thalia threw another kick my way. Evren and Sorin sat at the sides watching us. The two of them had just finished sparring and sweat dripped down Evren's bare chest.

Every time my gaze wandered in his direction, Thalia would land another blow.

"Ow!" I hissed as she hit my left thigh.

"Pay attention." Thalia laughed. "If you're distracted by him half naked, I would hate to see you in a real battle."

Evren chuckled, and I straightened my spine.

"I am not distracted by him."

"You could've fooled me." Thalia gave me a look that was a challenge.

"Shut up, and just go again."

Thalia smiled before correcting her stance. She watched me, looking for a weakness, before her legs shot out to the right. This time, I was able to block her and land my own kick to her stomach.

She grunted before grinning. "Good." She rubbed her hand across her abdomen. "That was much better."

"Add your power!" Evren called out, and my gaze met his. "She needs to work on controlling her power when there are other things to concentrate on as well."

I hated his words even though he was right. I hated how easily he could pick up my flaws.

"Don't you two have something better to do?" I didn't look at either of them as they snickered at my question.

"And miss this? I wouldn't dare." I could practically hear the smile in Evren's voice.

"Again." Thalia nodded at me once, and I could see the unspoken words in her eyes. *Show them exactly what you're made of.*

I nodded back at her as I widened my stance just like she taught me to. Sparring with Thalia was difficult. I had to feel her magic rather than see it. I tried to clear my mind, not think of Evren sitting at the side watching me, as I tried to concentrate on nothing but her.

A blast of her magic shot out, aiming directly for my chest, and I raised my hands and hit it with my own magic before it could make contact. Black smoke poured from my fingers, but I didn't have time to celebrate. Another shot of her magic came at me from the left, and I blocked it once more.

She smiled at me as she took a deep breath, but then I could feel her magic again surging stronger than before. I pivoted on my heel just as I realized it wasn't coming from her, and I shot my own magic out toward Evren and stopped his in its tracks. Sweat dripped down my temples as he grinned.

"Good. You're getting much better at detecting magic." There was a gleam in Evren's eyes as he held my gaze.

"I didn't realize you were going to be stabbing me in the back with yours."

"In the real world, no one's going to care if you're looking at them or if you're ready." He pushed to his feet and dusted off his trousers. "You have to train yourself to be ready for whatever comes your way."

I nodded because I knew he was right. "Your magic is easier to detect than Thalia's."

The smile that took over his face was wicked, and my stomach tightened as I looked upon him. "That's because you're my mate." He took a few steps closer to me. "Our magic is linked, so you will be able to feel my magic much easier than anyone else's."

"How else is our magic linked?"

"I don't know." He took another step closer and black smoke trailed from his fingers. "It is legend that mates could pull power from one another in time of need, that you could take from me or I could pull from you, but I've never seen it done. Mates are rare, and mates with magic that is linked so intricately as ours is even rarer."

"So what does that mean?" My heart hammered in my chest as I watched his magic, and my own surged inside of me begging to feel him.

"It means that we will have to figure this out as we go." He shrugged his shoulders. "Mates have always been more powerful together, and their marriage only strengthens that power. We will figure out what we're capable of based on the decisions that we make."

"You mean if I agree to marry?" I put my hands on my hips even as the words that just passed my lips thrilled me.

Evren's gaze fell upon them, and his smile never left his face. "That's exactly what I mean, princess. Legend says you will determine the fate of this world, but you will determine far more than that."

"That she will." Jorah pushed through the door, and Thalia took off in his direction. She ran toward him, jumping straight into his arms, and he caught her with a large smile on his face.

"You're back." Thalia seemed to breathe a sigh of relief, and Jorah tightened his arms around her.

I looked at Sorin, and a smile formed on his lips even as his shoulders tightened.

Thalia squeezed him again before dropping back to her feet and running her hands over his face and down his chest.

"You have word?" Evren asked, and Jorah simply held up a black scroll with a gold seal.

"Queen Kaida clearly knows more than we thought. Her men hand-delivered this to us this morning. Right where we were meant to be spying on the kingdom."

Evren stepped forward and grabbed the parchment from Jorah's hand, and I watched him as he unrolled it and looked over it. His hands gripped the sides so tightly that the parchment crinkled in his fingers, and I could feel his power surge and surge as his eyes scanned over the words.

"What is it?" Sorin stood and moved to Evren's side. "Fuck." Sorin looked at me, but all I could concentrate on was Evren. His magic felt stronger than I had ever felt before. It was pure and unfiltered, and it felt like rage.

"What's wrong?" I asked, and Evren's gaze flew to me. They were darker than they had seemed only moments before.

"It's from Gavril." The parchment crumpled in his hands.

"And?" My chest tightened, and I was desperate for him to just tell me what was going on.

"And he's sent me an official invitation to his wedding?"

"His wedding?" I looked back and forth between him and Sorin. "To whom?"

"My mate." He practically spat the words. "He fucking dares to send me an invitation to his supposed wedding with you."

"This is nothing more than a taunt." Thalia moved close to Evren and read the invitation over his shoulder. "He's trying to get under your skin."

"This is a threat." Evren stared directly at me, and I could feel his anger as if it was a living, breathing thing. "He thinks that he's going to take Adara back."

"We won't allow that to happen," Jorah promised, and the certainty in his voice begged me to believe him. "We won't let him close to her."

Evren wasn't listening to them, though. His attention was solely on me. "His name is next to yours." Black smoke trickled from his fingers, and I knew he was no longer in control of himself. "He requests the honor of my presence at the marriage of their crowned prince and the Starblessed who was promised."

"I need a moment," I said quietly, and Evren shook his head.

"Fuck no."

But I wasn't talking to him, and I looked past him to look at his friends. "I need a moment with my mate," I said it more firmly, and the three of them looked to Evren before looking back at me.

"Okay." Thalia nodded before grabbing Jorah's hand. "Let's give them some space."

I waited as all three of them left the small courtyard that had felt more like home to me than almost anywhere else. My hands trembled as Evren stared at me. Neither his anger nor his magic had calmed, and I could feel them reaching for me as if I was the only thing capable of settling them.

"That invitation means nothing."

His gaze darkened at my words and his fingers dug harder into the invitation. "You think threatening my mate is nothing?"

"I think that his threats don't matter. I am your mate, and I am here with you in the Blood kingdom." I motioned my hand toward the parchment. "What can that little piece of parchment do?"

"It will instill fear." He stepped closer to me, and a chill ran down the markings along my spine. "When news of this spreads, it will instill fear in my people and in so many people who remain in the fae kingdom. They will fear war and the possibility that Gavril could gain power over both kingdoms."

"The fae kingdom doesn't support Gavril?"

"Those people have never supported Gavril or his mother. They have seen their cruelty, and most don't care that your betrothal will strengthen their kingdom. Gavril needs no more power at his fingertips."

"Then don't give it to him."

"What?" He looked furious as he searched my face, and I realized that this was about so much more than Gavril's power. Gavril had threatened his mate. He had threatened me. "How do you suppose I do that?"

"We send an invitation of our own." I straightened my spine and tried to keep my voice from shaking.

He went stock-still as he stared at me. "An invitation?"

"Yes." I nodded and tried to keep my nerves from rushing through me. "I'm obviously not marrying Gavril, and he just wants to make people believe that. Give them the truth and send an invitation for our own."

"But you and I aren't getting married."

"Aren't we?" I cocked my head and studied him. "You asked for my hand, did you not?"

"Yes." He watched me carefully. "And you turned me down. Several times."

"And I change my mind."

"Not like this." He shook his head, and I could see the indecision running through him. "I don't want you to say yes because of this."

"It's not—"

"It isn't an option," he cut me off, and my power surged inside of me. He was really and truly angry, but there was also so much worry in his eyes. This was a threat he was taking seriously. "We will figure something else out."

"I won the bet."

"What?" He ran his hand over the back of his head as he stared back down at the invitation. With every flick of his gaze, I could feel his power soaring higher.

"Last night you said that if I won then you owed me. Whatever I chose, it would be mine."

Evren's gaze snapped to mine, but he didn't say a word.

"This is what I want. This is what you owe me." I crossed my arms and hoped he realized just how serious I was. "I want to marry you."

"Adara," he sighed my name as he shook his head.

"You said that you didn't want to force me to do anything. You didn't want to take my choice, so don't." My breaths rushed in and out of me. "This is my choice, Evren, and I choose you."

He watched me for a long moment before stepping closer to me ever so carefully. His anger hadn't softened, but there was also desire flowing along his power. His hunger was stifling and almost choked out the rage that coursed through him.

"This isn't a game, princess."

"I never said it was." My own anger spiked. "You are my mate, and I am yours. I choose to marry you, Evren. This was what you wanted before. Why do you not want me now?"

He surged forward, his body slamming into mine, and the invitation was lost on the ground behind him. "Never say that again." His fingers trailed over my face before cupping my cheeks.

I stared up at him with ragged breaths passing my lips and waited for his next words.

"I will always want you, Adara. I have since the moment I met you." His gaze ran over the length of my face. "But I don't want to force a decision out of you because of my brother. That invitation doesn't mean you need to decide anything."

"Yes. It does." I nodded with my head still in his hands. "You and I both know it."

He closed his eyes as he bit down on his bottom lip, and I

could feel his emotions warring in his powers. It was still so out of control, and I didn't think he realized how much he was allowing me.

"I want to marry you, Evren. I want to be by your side. We will do this together."

His mouth came down against mine, softly and unsure, and his lips traced over mine as if they were trying to memorize the curve. "I am yours, Adara."

"And I am yours."

My chest tightened as the words passed through my lips, and I didn't know the power that they held.

"I need you," he murmured against my lips and started backing us up toward the palace wall.

"Shouldn't we tell the others our plan?" My chest felt tight and my stomach churned. I wasn't second-guessing my decisions, but I wasn't sure I was ready for this. This intimacy that Evren was staring at me with.

"No." He shook his head, and his hands hit the stone wall right before my back hit them. "I just need you."

He moved his hands over me, caressing and wandering, and he didn't stop until he held my face and forced me to look up at him. "You are mine, and I will worship you until my last breath is stolen from my body."

"Evren," I whispered his name and tried to look away from him, but he refused to let me go.

"I am devoted to you, princess." He lowered his hand down my neck until he pressed it against my chest. "To your mind, your body."

"And to your people," I reminded him. "Our marriage will strengthen your kingdom and ensure safety for your people."

"*Our* people, *our* kingdom." His other hand pushed in my hair, and he gripped the roots and forced me to look back up at him.

I nodded even as my heart raced, and I wasn't sure how I felt.

"Kiss me, princess," he demanded of me. There was no asking, no hesitancy from him, and there wasn't a single part of me that was capable of denying him.

He leaned forward to close the space between us, but his attention caught on my chest, and he stiffened against me. He lifted his hand to my neck, and his finger dipped beneath the chain of my necklace and lifted it.

I slammed my hand down over his, trying to stop him, but he had already seen it.

"Where did you get this?"

"I'm sorry." I scrambled and put my hand over the small moon. I hadn't thought about it when I slipped it over my head this morning. It had been tucked inside my shirt while I sparred, and no one had noticed. Not until now. "I'll give it back."

I started to lift it off me, but his hands stopped my own.

"Where did you get it?"

"Your room." I pulled my attention away from him as a blush crept up my neck. "I found it on your desk while you were gone. It had my name on it."

He didn't say anything. He just stared down at the gold chain that lay against my skin.

"I'm sorry, Evren. I know I shouldn't have taken it." I shook my head and once again tried to move, but he wouldn't let me.

"Do you know what that is?" His gaze finally met mine, and nausea rolled through me.

"No." I shook my head. "I saw it, and I don't know. I felt drawn to it somehow."

Evren was quiet for a long moment, and my anxiety soared with every moment of his silence.

"I'm sorry. I didn't mean to…"

"That belonged to your father."

"What?" I pushed my hands against his chest and shot my power into him and pushed him away.

"It's your father's," Evren repeated himself, but his words didn't make sense. None of it did.

I pressed my hands against my own chest, against where the pendant laid, and I could feel the slight buzz of it beneath my skin.

"You're lying." I shook my head. "Why would you lie to me about this?"

"Queen Kaida gave it to Gavril to give to you as a gift. It was one more way for them to use you, to manipulate you. He was going to gift it to you on your wedding night." Evren's anger surged along with his uncertainty.

"And how do you have it? Why do you have my father's pendant?" There was so much accusation in my voice. Accusation that I didn't understand, but I also couldn't let go of.

"I stole it. The night Gavril fed from you, the night we left, I stole it from his room before we disappeared under the night sky."

"And what? You are just going to use it against me as well?"

Evren stepped back as if my words harmed him, but I couldn't stop. This pendant belonged to my father. I could feel it in my bones that it was the truth, but I also knew that Evren's family only had it because it was taken from him against his will.

It was taken from him when they killed my father.

"Do you really think so little of me?" He ran his hands through his hair. "Do you really think that I could be capable of hurting you in such a way?"

I shook my head as I clung to the pendant and thought after thought raced through my mind. Thoughts of my father, thoughts about me. I could do nothing but race over everything that I had once thought I was sure of, but doubt had become my biggest enemy.

Because when I stared ahead at my mate, doubt raced through every part of me.

"I stole the necklace to take their power away. I stole you to take their power away." Evren stepped forward, and I watched him carefully. "It was foolish of me to do so, princess. To go to my brother's room and steal something from him that I knew he would miss. He knew that I took it. The queen knew, and it was a risk I shouldn't have taken. But I took it for you."

I tried to swallow down my emotions as my fingers burned against the pendant. "Why didn't you give it to me? Why would you wait?"

"Because you didn't trust me." Evren ran his hand down his chest, and I could see the plea in his eyes for me to believe him. "You didn't trust me, and I didn't want you to think that I would ever use such a thing against you. My father and his queen have taken everything from you. This is the only thing I could get back." He shook his head as he stared at me. "I didn't want you to ever think that I would use it against you to force your hand into marrying me. I left it on my desk with your name on it in case anything was to happen to me while I was gone. I still wanted you to have it."

"No more secrets." My hands trembled as I straightened my spine and tried to force myself not to look weak. "I have agreed to this marriage, but there can be no more secrets."

"Of course." Evren's hand tightened in his shirt. "Of course, princess. Anything you want."

"Why did my father wear this pendant?" I fingered the crescent moon as I asked.

"I don't know, but Queen Kaida was adamant that she could use it to sway you. She was adamant that Gavril could use it against you if he had to."

"I can feel it." I looked up at him, and he was still watching me. "That was how I found it on your desk. I could feel its power."

"I can too." Evren reached forward and laid his hand upon

mine. "Which makes me believe that the queen knew as well. I'm worried that she knows things that we don't."

"Things about my father?" *Desperate.* I felt so hopelessly desperate for his answer.

"Things about him. Things about you. I don't know." His hand tightened against mine, and I could feel his fear trembling through him.

I didn't know my father. I hardly knew any details of his life other than the sacrifice he made for me. I pressed my hand against the pendant as the agony of wishing I did hit me.

"We should tell the others our plan."

Evren's gaze met mine, and his eyes darkened as he clenched his jaw. He wanted me alone, just him and me, but our reality was too dire for that.

Everything that was happening was far more than just the two of us.

It always had been.

"You're right." He nodded and slipped my hand in his. "We should discuss our next move."

He hesitated for a long moment with my hand in his. If it could have been this, just him and me, things would have been so much different.

It would have been more than I could have ever dreamed.

"Let's go." He pulled me forward, and I held my hand in his while my other still clutched the pendant on my neck.

SEVENTEEN

I hadn't seen Evren since yesterday.

After we told the others of our plan, he was whisked away to talk strategy with his mother and her advisors. He had offered for me to come, but I had refused.

I still didn't trust the woman, and thoughts were swirling in my mind about my father and the pendant that still buzzed against my chest. There was also the fact that I couldn't get the image of the way Evren's friends, my friends, had all lit up with the news of our betrothal. Thalia had grinned exceptionally hard, and Sorin cursed under his breath with a smile on his face as he slid something into Thalia's hand.

I had just needed a moment to breathe.

My feet bounced on the floor as I sat on the edge of the bed and stared at the door. Mina had brought me dinner before quickly leaving, and she had let me know that she was serving Evren his meal in the throne room.

I looked to my feet then back to the door. The sun had fallen and the moons had taken its place, and I knew I should have just laid down and gone to sleep.

But I couldn't.

My heart was beating at the same anxious rhythm that my feet bounced against the hard floor, and no matter what I did, I couldn't seem to calm myself down.

I climbed from the bed and pulled the small throw blanket around me. I was wearing nothing but a shirt and my undergarments, but I just needed a peek. To see if he was back in his room.

I opened my door before slowly creeping across the hall, and I leaned my ear against Evren's door. Silence. I heard nothing from the other side, and my stomach tightened as I looked down the hall.

I should have gone back to my room and waited until tomorrow, but I didn't. I tiptoed down the hall, and I didn't stop until I made my way into the main entryway. A few soldiers stood there, and they were taking direction from Jorah. His gaze snapped up to meet me as I entered the large room, and he said a few more words to them before making his way to me.

"Is everything okay?" His voice was firm, all business just like I had known Jorah to be.

"Are you okay?" I tightened the blanket around me. "I've barely spoken to you since you returned."

Jorah's face softened, and he took a step closer to me. "I'm fine, Adara. You need not worry for me."

I looked down the hallway which I knew led toward the kitchens.

"Is there something else?"

I looked back toward him. "Where's the throne room?"

Jorah smiled, and I hated the blush I could feel rising up my chest. But it didn't matter that he knew I was looking for his prince. Evren was my mate and my soon-to-be husband, and I needed to get over the fact that people would know I wanted him.

"Right this way." He motioned me forward, and I followed him down the long hallway.

"He's been in here all day." There was an edge of concern in Jorah's voice.

"What exactly is he working on?"

"Ensuring that there's no way his brother can get to you. It's his only concern. You are his priority."

I nodded in understanding even as my chest tightened.

Jorah stopped near a large set of double doors. They were grander than the rest, the tops curved in a beautiful arch that met an intricate design of vines and a sword in the middle.

Jorah knocked twice before he pushed the door open. I took a deep breath and held the blanket tightly around me before stepping inside. There was a large dais at one end of the room with two thrones upon it. Both as black as night and twin in design.

But Evren sat at a large table that was taking up most of the room, and he was staring down at parchments of maps in front of him. There were a few others in the room as well as both Thalia and Sorin at his sides, but it was only him I could see.

He hadn't noticed me yet, but Thalia did. She gave me a small smile as she stood from her chair and nodded toward Sorin.

He looked up from the maps he was studying with Evren, and he blinked when he saw me standing in the corner of the room. He started to move from the table, and Evren's attention finally pulled away from the maps and landed on me.

He looked like he hadn't slept since yesterday. His eyes were dark and tired, and his hair was disheveled as if he had been running his hands through it.

"Princess." He stood from his chair without taking his eyes off me. "Did you need something?"

I hated how tired he looked. How worn down he was over his racing thoughts of keeping me safe. And I wanted to take them away.

"It's late." I let my gaze fall to the windows that stood beyond the dais. "Why don't you get some rest?"

I saw Evren's face falter, and he sat back down in his chair. "I will rest. But there are some things I need to attend to first."

Thalia looked back and forth between us, but I couldn't make out the look on her face.

But it didn't matter. It didn't matter what anyone in the room thought other than him, and I pulled my blanket tighter around me as I made my way to him. He leaned back in his chair as he watched me, his hands gripping the arms of the chair.

"Adara." Even his voice sounded so tired.

"Evren." I mocked the way he said my name, and Sorin chuckled at his side.

"I think Adara is right." He walked past Evren before reaching me and placing a kiss on my forehead. "We've been at it all night and day. We could all do with some rest."

Evren nodded once even as he gritted his teeth. It wasn't what he wanted to hear, but I stood silently as Thalia and Sorin left the room along with the other soldiers that had been at their sides. The large doors closed with a loud thud, but I didn't take my eyes off of Evren.

"I don't need rest." His voice was taut, and he looked along the maps in front of him. "There is far too much to worry about than to think of rest."

"People tend to make mistakes when they're tired." I held the blanket tighter around me and ran the soft fabric against my chin.

Evren cocked an eyebrow at me, and I could see the ghost of a smile on his lips. "You think I'm going to make mistakes?"

"I didn't say that." I took a small step closer to him. "But you look exhausted."

"Ah." He chuckled. "My betrothed is worried that I won't look good on her arm?"

My stomach tightened at hearing him call me that, and I couldn't seem to make my hands quit trembling.

I forced myself between him and the table, and I didn't stop until I was standing between his thighs. He pushed his head back against his chair and stared up at me.

"I'm not sure that there's anything you could do to make you not look good." I pushed my fingers into his hair, and his eyes closed at my touch.

He leaned forward and slid his hand beneath the blanket. His fingers touched my bare thigh, and his gaze darkened.

"Are you telling me that you're attracted to me?" His lips curved at the side, and my chest loosened at the sight.

"I would never admit such a thing."

He laughed and his hands moved around the backs of my thighs. "Oh, princess." His grip tightened, and he lifted me as I let out a small squeal.

He didn't stop until my ass hit the edge of the table, and my hands came down and had most of his maps flying to the floor.

"Your stuff."

"It'll be fine." He leaned forward and pushed his body between my thighs. "I have more important things to attend to."

"Like what?" I barely managed to breathe out the words.

"My mate," he growled and jerked me forward until my sex pressed against his chest. "It would appear that she needs me."

"I don't think I said I needed you." My blanket was barely covering me anymore, but I still clung to it like it could save me.

"No, but the scent of you tells me otherwise." His hands ran along my thighs, and I attempted to close them around him as I blushed.

"That's not true."

"Isn't it?" He stared down at my thighs as his fingers trailed over the inside, just over my scar. "Are you telling me if I go just a little bit higher, I won't find you soaking?"

"I came in here to check on you." I looked back toward the door. "I wanted to make sure that you were okay."

His face softened, but his hands didn't. "I'm fine, princess."

"You don't look fine. You look worried."

"I am worried." He nodded once before leaning forward and pressing a kiss to the inside of my knee.

"I would be foolish not to be."

"What can I do?"

He leaned back in his chair and stared at me once again. "Nothing, Adara. You've already given enough. I just need to figure out what they're planning."

"You'll drive yourself mad." I shook my head. "You can't control everything, Evren. You can't predict what it is that they'll do next."

His gaze hardened. "You are my mate, and it is my promise to protect you. I will not break that promise."

His words were heavy and true, and I could see how much they weighed upon him.

I pushed forward from the table, and I didn't stop until I pushed onto his lap and pressed a knee to the chair on either side of his thighs. I wrapped my hands into the hair at the back of his head and forced him to look up at me.

"You cannot protect me from everything, Evren." I tugged on the strands of his hair as the blanket fell from my shoulders. "You are not responsible for shielding me from every possible harm."

His hands settled on my hips and grasped my shirt in their grip. "I can't explain it, princess." His hands tugged me closer. "When I read your name on that invitation, I felt dangerous. I lost control of who I'm supposed to be."

"And who exactly are you supposed to be?" I searched his dark eyes even as my body ached with the desire to be closer to him.

"More."

I shook my head at his absurdity. "You are foolish then." I leaned closer to him until my lips were a whisper against his.

"Adara," he sighed my name, and my magic swirled with fear of him pushing me away.

I pressed my lips harder against him, kissing him with every bit of need that had been building inside of me.

"If you won't rest, let me take some of your burden from you." I kissed along his jaw. "Use me to clear your mind. Drown in me until you can think of nothing else."

His hands tightened on my hips, and he tugged me forward until my sex slammed against him. A whimper passed through my lips and landed upon his.

"I can't be gentle right now, princess," he rumbled against my lips. "I need to work."

I leaned away from him, but I wasn't going to let him do this. If he couldn't be gentle then I would handle whatever it was he would throw my way, but I couldn't leave him here with that haunted look in his eyes.

I slowly unbuttoned my shirt as he watched me. My fingers were sure, and I watched as his breath rushed in and out of him.

"What are you doing?" His voice was smoky and did little to calm my racing heart.

I opened the button at the bottom of my belly before letting my shirt fall open. I felt so exposed in front of him, but my stomach tightened in anticipation.

"You may not need me, but I need you." I ran my fingers over my neck before letting them fall down my chest and stomach. I held his gaze as I slowly pushed them inside my undergarments.

I whimpered against my touch, and gods, I was already so wet.

Evren was stoic beneath me, but his chest rose and fell quickly. He didn't look away from me for even a moment.

I dipped my fingers into my wetness before moving it over my nub, and I grasped his forearm and ground down against him as pleasure shot through me.

My eyes fluttered, and I wanted to close them as lust swelled inside me but I refused. I kept my eyes on him as he watched me, and I could feel how hard he was beneath me.

"You think I don't need you?" he gritted the words through his teeth, and I ground down harder against him.

My hips rolled in rhythm with my fingers, and his knuckles turned white against the chair.

"It would appear so." My thighs tightened around him as another surge of pleasure flowed through me. "You hardly seem affected by me."

I slipped my fingers from my undergarments and brought them up to my mouth. I could see the moisture coating my fingers, and I kept my eyes on him as I placed them against my lips and ran my tongue along the tips.

Evren's gaze darkened, and I could almost see the moment he snapped. He snatched my wrist in his hand, pulling it away from my mouth, and he groaned long and loudly when his tongue met mine.

"Fuck," he cursed against my mouth, and his hands tightened around me.

He lifted me, pushing me back down against the table, and his fingers gripped the sides of my undergarments before he ripped them down my thighs. I lifted off the table, helping him pull them all the way off, and his gaze was glued to my sex.

Moisture pooled between my legs as he moved to the edge of his chair and forced my knees apart. He didn't give me a moment to adjust or to come to my senses. He wrapped his arms beneath each of my thighs and jerked me forward until my ass hung off the side of the table and I landed back on my elbows.

"As if there is anything you could do that I wouldn't be affected by." He ran his nose along the length of my thigh, and I looked up at the ceiling. "My desire for you destroys every bit of my loyalty to my duty."

His lips met my sex, and I gasped.

His tongue ran along the length of me, and he groaned. "Fuck, you're so fucking wet."

My gaze met his, and he didn't look away from me as he ate from my flesh.

"Eyes on me, princess," he growled against my skin just as he slipped two fingers inside of me.

I whimpered and tried to tighten my thighs, but he refused to allow it. He pinned me open with one of his hands on my thighs, and his other began pumping in and out of me just as he sucked my nub softly into his mouth.

"Oh, gods."

"Don't call out to them." His fingers dug into my thigh, and his other fingers curled inside me. "I am the one who is worshipping you. I will worship at this altar until you are ripped from my fingers."

My back bowed from the table as pleasure swelled inside me, and my chest trembled as I tried to take in a breath.

"I want every moan that passes your lips to be a result of my touch. I want what you feel for me to burn inside of you until you have no choice but to let it out." He pressed his lips against my nub, and my hips surged off the table. "I want to get so lost in each other that we forget everything else if even for a moment."

I cursed under my breath, and Evren's fingers slid away from my skin. I searched his gaze as I watched him open his trousers and lean back in his chair. He reached forward, gripping my thighs in his hands, and he lifted me until I had no choice but to cling to his arms and allow him to move me back to his lap.

My legs spread around him, and he held his cock as he lined it up with my sex and pulled me down over him. I bit down on my lip as he stretched me, and I pressed my hands against his shoulders.

"Fuck, you feel so good." He pressed his head back against the chair and stared up at me as his hands guided my hips until I was fully seated against him. "Do you feel how perfectly you take me?"

I nodded as I rolled my hips against him. My marks buzzed and craved his touch just as much as the magic inside me. Both were desperate for him, as desperate as I felt, and when he lifted my hips in his hands and slammed me back down against him, I buried my head in his neck to try to keep myself from begging him for more.

His hips rolled beneath me as he wrapped an arm around my back, and he used the leverage of his body beneath mine to slam back inside of me over and over until I couldn't think let alone breathe.

He pressed his lips to my shoulders, groaning against my skin as he held me closer to him. There was room between us to hide the fact that my body trembled against his as our hips moved together.

Evren gathered my hair in his hand, and he pulled my head back until I was forced to look at him. "No hiding, princess. I want to strip you bare. I want to see every part of you."

He never stopped moving as he watched me, his gaze peering into mine, and I felt so exposed. My body was on edge, every part of me was watching him watch me, and the look in his eyes only heightened everything.

"You are my mate," he growled as he thrust into me. I could feel my pleasure teetering at the precipice, waiting to fall over the edge. "You are my everything."

I swallowed hard as I searched his face. He held my gaze firmly, and I had nowhere to hide from his truth.

"Say it." His hand tightened in my hair as he continued to thrust inside of me. "Say you're mine."

"I'm yours." My hands trembled against his shoulders and wave after wave of pleasure hit me. "And you are mine."

"I will never let him take you." He wrapped an arm around

my back and pulled me tighter against him. "He will never touch you again."

His voice shook with his promise. Evren would choose me.

If it came down to me and his kingdom, something deep in my chest told me that he would choose me.

My fingers tightened on his shoulders and my magic slithered inside me. Black smoke fell from my fingers against his skin, and the groan that fell from his lips was a deep rumble as I began rolling my hips harder against him.

My body felt like I was burning, like I was on the verge of combusting, and I chased that feeling even though I knew I shouldn't.

"Evren," I whispered his name, and I needed to know that he was falling apart with me.

"That's it, princess." His lips moved to my neck, and he grazed his teeth along my sensitive skin. "Ride me."

His hand moved and gripped my breast tightly in his fingers.

"You take me so fucking good," he whispered against my neck. "Your body fits mine so perfectly. You feel that?"

I nodded my head against him as I bit down on my bottom lip. My pleasure was surging inside me, begging me to let go, and I feared I might drown when I finally did.

It was too much, the way I felt about Evren, and it was all crashing into me.

"I have never wanted anything more, princess." His tongue ran against my ear. "I have never felt so desperate to give someone else this kind of pleasure."

"I'm so close," I whimpered, and his hands moved to my hips.

He lifted me, just a few inches off of him before he slammed me back down against him. I moaned as he hit something inside me that I was desperate for.

"Good girl." His nose ran along my jaw. "Let go for me. Give me what is mine."

I wanted to. I had never wanted anything more, but I dug into him and my magic poured from my fingers. I was looking over the edge, desperate to fall, but I couldn't.

I couldn't let go even though I was screaming at myself to do it in my head.

Evren's teeth grazed over my neck once more, and my core tightened around him. "Can I?"

I nodded my head just as his tongue met my neck.

"I need your words, princess. You have to tell me it's what you want."

"Please," I begged him. "Please, Evren."

The words had barely passed my lips when his teeth sank into my skin. Pain sliced through me, and my body froze against him. But that pain was quickly replaced with pleasure, and I let my head fall back, giving my mate more access to me.

His teeth sank deeper into me, and his hands tightened on my hips. He lifted me higher before pulling me back into him, and my body sparked with pleasure.

Pleasure that wouldn't stop.

"Evren!" I cried out his name, and his hips surged from the chair.

His own magic fell from his hands and floated along my skin as we moved together. His hands were tense against my body, and his magic felt reckless against me.

He thrust inside me once more with a loud groan against my skin, and my core clamped down around him as I felt his own pleasure spill over inside me. I could no longer hold on, no longer chase the feeling, because it slammed into me, throwing me off the edge.

And I lost control as I came against him.

He pulled his teeth from my neck before bringing his mouth to mine, and I could taste my blood on his lips. I should have pulled away, been disgusted by the act, but I kissed him harder than I ever had before.

Pleasure still rushed through every inch of me, and I didn't want to stop and think about why I was so aroused by my mate taking from me.

He had only done so before when there was a dire need, but this was different. This need was nothing more than primal, and my hands shook against him as I tried to come down from the high it gave me. This wasn't about saving anyone. This was me choosing every part of him.

I pulled back from him and stared at my mate. His face was flushed and his gaze lazy, and I could no longer see worry rolling off him as I had before.

"Are you okay?" His voice was tired as he ran his fingers over my neck where he had just bitten.

I nodded and ran my fingers down his arms. My magic still trickled from my fingers, but it was softer now, more controlled.

"I want you in my bed tonight."

My gaze flew up to his. "What?"

He pushed my hair out of my face and searched for something I was unsure of. "You are my mate, and now you are my betrothed. You will be in my bed from now on."

"That isn't very proper."

Evren snorted, and I couldn't help but smile.

"I don't think the way you just took me was very proper either, princess." He leaned forward and ran his nose along my collarbone. "Nothing I wish to do to you is very proper."

I swallowed hard, and my thighs tightened around him.

"You like that, princess? You like thinking about all the ways your mate dreams of defiling you?"

I didn't say a word as he looked back up at me and pulled my bottom lip in between his teeth. They scraped over the sensitive skin, and another small wave of pleasure coursed through me.

Evren chuckled before pressing a small kiss to the side of my mouth. "Gods, you're going to destroy me."

EIGHTEEN

I awoke to the sound of knocking at the door, and I had barely managed to peek an eye open when Evren called for whomever it was to come in.

Thalia pushed through the door with a worried look on her face and a small parchment in her hand.

I pressed my hand to Evren's chest as I sat up and pulled his sheet to my chest.

"There's news." She held the parchment in his direction before her gaze slid to me.

"What is it?" Evren leaned forward and took the parchment from her hand.

"It's reported that three dozen fae soldiers ride toward our border."

"What?" Evren pushed his hair out of his face before quickly opening the parchment. His chest was bare and the sheet fell to his hips. Every bit of the worry that had disappeared from his face last night was back full force, and I tightened my hand in the sheet as I watched him.

"They say that Gavril rides with them."

Evren's gaze darted from the parchment to look up at our friend. "That's impossible."

I could see it then, the tense posture in Thalia's shoulders, the way her jaw clenched almost unnoticeably. She was strong, stronger than almost anyone I had ever met, but she was rightfully fearful of the man who had used her. I was fearful of him too.

"What does this mean?"

Evren looked at me as he worked his lip between his teeth. He didn't say a word. He just looked back down at the parchment in his hand as his other slid over to mine.

He gripped my fingers in his as he read the words that were inked on the parchment, and I could feel his anger rising with each passing second.

"It would appear that my brother would like to find a compromise." His fingers tightened around the parchment. "He is coming to offer me something in exchange for you."

"What?" I looked back and forth between him and Thalia, and she could barely meet my gaze. "What could he possibly have to trade?"

"I don't know." Evren shook his head before letting go of my hand and climbing out of bed. He pulled his trousers on quickly before pulling a shirt over his head. "But we need to figure it out. We need to prepare for anything with his arrival."

"He's a threat." It wasn't a question.

"My brother will always be a threat, princess, and the fact that he's coming here himself is dangerous. I don't like not knowing what to expect."

He pulled on a boot before sitting down and quickly tugging the other up his leg.

"Are you all right, Thalia?"

Her gaze slammed into mine, and her eyes widened at my question. She looked like she had been so deep in her own mind that she had forgotten either of us were in the room.

"Yes." She nodded once. "Of course."

But she wasn't. There was no way that she could be. She hadn't seen Gavril since she escaped from the fae kingdom, but I was sure that she thought of him. I was positive that she dreamed of him and his horror in a way that I couldn't fathom.

"Get everyone in the throne room, including my mother." Evren nodded toward her. "We need to prepare before they arrive."

"Of course." Thalia turned quickly and left the room without another word.

Evren stood and tucked his shirt into his trousers before rolling up his sleeves. He grabbed something from his desk, tucking it in his pocket, and my worry spiked as I watched him.

"Evren," I called his name softly, but he didn't stop. He was pacing his room, gathering his dagger before strapping it to his side. "Evren."

I was firmer this time, and he finally stopped to look at me.

"You should get dressed." His gaze fell to my naked body, that was only shielded by his sheet. "We'll need you, too."

"Okay," I agreed, but I made no move to do as he said.

"Adara."

My gaze snapped up to meet his at the sound of my name, and I pressed the sheet against my chest. There was so much anger and fear in his eyes, and my chest tightened as I saw it.

"There's nothing he can do." My voice shook as I climbed to my knees. "You and I are to be married, and there is nothing he can do."

Evren shook his head as he watched me. "I wish that were true, but we both know that he's capable of things we can't even fathom. I fear what he has if he thinks I would be willing to trade you for it."

"He doesn't know." I caught myself before I said something stupid and swallowed hard. "He has no idea that I intend to marry you."

His gaze darkened, and he closed the space between us with a few short steps. "He doesn't know how I feel about you." He leaned down and pressed his fists into the mattress, his face mere inches from mine. "Is that what you mean to say?"

I opened my mouth to answer, but I felt foolish. I slowly shook my head, but Evren reached forward and caught my jaw in his hand. He held it firmly until I was forced to look up at him.

"Because you are right. He doesn't have a clue." His thumb ran along my bottom lip. "There is nothing in this world or the next that he can offer me that would make me be willing to give you up. He cannot cause me to falter in what I feel for you, princess."

I couldn't catch my breath. I could hardly remember to do anything other than beg him to stay as I stared up at him.

"Get dressed and let's head to the throne room. We shouldn't be ill-prepared when he arrives."

"Okay." I nodded, but neither of us made a move to leave.

He was still so close, still watching me, and his finger still roamed over my lip.

"Princess," he groaned softly, and my gaze fell to his lips.

"Promise me." I reached a hand out and wrapped it around the back of his neck. The sheet fell from my chest, but I made no move to fix it as I pulled him closer to me. "Promise me that no matter what he says, you won't let him take me."

It was selfish to ask that of him. Selfish for me to even think, but I couldn't stop the fear that was coursing through every inch of me.

He leaned closer until his mouth pressed against mine. "I swear it." His words were a murmur against my lips. "With all that I am, princess, I swear that he will never touch you again. I will stop at nothing to keep you safe."

My hands trembled against him, and every breath felt like it took effort as I held him to me. "I don't want to be without you."

He groaned, and his hand tightened against my face. "Nor I you."

His lips pressed hard against mine, smothering the fear and worry with want, and I whimpered against his lips as my thighs pressed together.

This want I had for him, it was insistent and greedy. It was unlike anything I had ever felt before.

I knew if we gave in to this want, we would never leave the room. We would be exactly as he feared. Completely unprepared for his brother's arrival.

"We should go and meet everyone."

Evren nodded against me, but the way he lingered told me he was as hesitant to leave me as I was him. In this room, in these moments we had alone, there was nothing but the two of us. The rest of the world is what destroyed us. It was the rest of the world that caused me to doubt.

But I couldn't bring that doubt to the surface of this moment. All I knew was I was his and he was mine, and he would do as he promised. He would protect me at all costs, and I was selfish for asking that of him.

I climbed out of bed quickly and threw on yesterday's clothes as Evren finished strapping weapons to his body. I slipped on my boots, and he held my dagger in my direction. I slid it into my boot before standing up next him and taking his hand in mine.

"You stay at my side." He tucked a piece of my hair behind my ear. "No matter what, you stay at my side."

I nodded because there was no way that I could leave him. Not now. Not with all this fear coursing through me. He was my safety, and I could feel it with every part of me.

We left his room hand in hand and made our way down to the throne room. Everyone was already inside sitting at the table, murmuring over maps and arguing over plans.

Mina and a few others were scurrying about the room, bringing in food and drink and placing them on the table. She looked flustered, her hands wringing against her apron and her normally pinned-back hair loose against her face. I stopped before her and let my hand slip from Evren's.

I grabbed her arms in my hands and bent until we were eye to eye. "Thank you, Mina."

She blinked up at me rapidly and her face turned ashen. I didn't know if it was fear for her kingdom or her prince or maybe even me, but it was fear just the same.

"I'm going to grab some tea." She pushed her hair her out of her face. "Everyone could use some calming tea." Her gaze searched the room, and I knew this was the only way Mina could help in that moment.

"That would be lovely."

She walked past me, and Evren snatched my hand back in his.

"Mina is scared," I whispered to him, and he nodded.

"Everyone is scared, princess. It is how we choose to use that fear that will define us. It is how we choose to use it that will determine the fate of our world."

Evren moved to the head of the table where only one chair remained. Queen Veda sat to his right with several of her men while Sorin, Thalia, and Jorah all sat to his left.

I took a step back and tried to pull my fingers from his, but he held me more firmly. "Sit."

He pulled out the chair at the head of the table, the chair that we had made love in mere hours ago, and I sat down where he asked me to. Queen Veda's wide gaze snapped up in my direction.

Evren moved to the other end of the table and grabbed a chair before bringing it back to me. He put the chair between his mother and me, and I felt like it was a clear divide on where I stood. There was his mother's side of the table with her men and then there was his. Sorin grabbed the arm of my chair and scooted me toward him with a loud scrape on the floor that made it evident where I belonged.

Evren sat down next to me, as tightly as the two of us could fit together, before looking at the parchments in front of him. "What do we know?"

Jorah spoke before anyone else could. "Gavril's men reached the outskirts of their land and delivered the parchment to one of our soldiers." He nodded to the parchment that lay before us. "He has three dozen men with him, and no others that we have been able to track. We're worried about an ambush, but there have been no signs that that's the truth."

"He can't be trusted." Queen Veda crossed her arms and leaned back in her chair. "I don't trust that he's coming here with only three dozen men. That would be a damning move for him."

"It would be if he deemed me capable of harming him." Evren reached forward and grabbed the parchment. He studied the writing, and I wondered what he was looking for. What signs he was searching for to find the truth behind his brother's lies. "He thinks that we hold no power and that him compromising with us will be seen as a gift."

Evren looked up from the parchment and looked around the table before his gaze finally settled on me. "My brother is much like his mother, and both have made a habit of underestimating me. We will use that weakness to our advantage."

Queen Veda looked unsure of what he said, and I didn't know if the worry that lay in her eyes was for her kingdom or for her son who was willing to sacrifice everything for it.

"We are going to tell him of your betrothal?" She looked back and forth between the two of us.

"We are." Evren tossed the parchment back down on the table and took my hand back in his. "The invitation that he sent was not only a threat to my mate, but a threat to me." His hand tightened in mine. "He wants me to fear what he is capable of, of what he's capable of taking from me, but he is the one who should fear me."

I looked over at Evren's circle of friends, and every one of them looked so proud of their prince. They looked so sure of his words and the truth that rang behind them, and I found myself believing every one of them as well.

"The two of you must make this believable." She looked back and forth between Evren and me. "Gavril must believe without a doubt that the two of you are in love and incapable of losing the other."

My back straightened, and I took in a sharp breath. I knew one of those things with absolute certainty. I was incapable of losing him. But it was the other that gave me pause. He was my mate, and I knew that I felt strongly for him. I felt more for him than I had ever felt for another, but I wasn't sure if that was love.

"Are you capable of that, Adara?"

I stared at the queen as I gripped Evren's hand firmly in mine. I could feel my magic swirling inside of me, my marks buzzing with the emotions that were running through me. "I am capable of whatever Evren asks of me." I lifted my chin and felt everyone's eyes on me. "I am his to command and his alone."

Her eyes narrowed and her back straightened as she watched me. "I am your queen."

I felt Evren's magic churn against my own, calling to me, coaxing me to behave, but it wasn't that simple.

"Evren is my mate. He is my prince and my future husband. You being my queen does not eclipse any of those facts. I will show Gavril that I am deeply devoted to my mate, because I am." I didn't let my gaze fall from hers. "Will others have trouble showing the same devotion?"

Queen Veda opened her mouth to speak, but I wasn't finished.

"A prince born of blood. Another of power," I quoted the prophecy to her that I hadn't been able to forget since Evren told me, and I saw her blink in confusion. "We are fighting a war of two queens, but the prophecy speaks of neither. The fate of our kingdom lies with your son, and it will be him and him alone who determines what role I play in it."

I finally let my gaze fall from her, and it fell back on Evren who was watching me. His gaze was dark and full of lust, and it made me ache with the memories of what he could do to me.

He raised my hand in his, his gaze never falling from mine, as he pressed his lips against my knuckles. My stomach fluttered, and my heart raced as I watched him.

"Gavril will believe that Adara belongs to me because it's the truth." Evren finally pulled his gaze away from me to look back at the others. "She belongs to me as much as I belong to her, and regardless of what my brother offers in compromise, I will not give her up."

"And are you ready to face the consequences of that decision?" The queen stared at her son, and I knew what she was asking. Was he prepared to choose me over his kingdom? Was he prepared to let down the people he had sacrificed his entire life to protect?

"There is no doubt in my mind over what I will choose." Evren's magic snaked along my palm. "So you ought to clear the doubt from yours and prepare yourself for war if that's what it takes. I will go to war for my kingdom, and I will go to war for my mate."

My chest tightened as I took in his words, as I took in the promise he had just delivered, but it was the next words that made me feel like I couldn't breathe.

"As will I." Thalia's voice was sure and left no room for argument. "I will choose Adara, and I will go to war for her if that's what it takes."

"As will I." Sorin nodded in my direction, and emotion welled up inside of me.

"Without question." Jorah held the queen's gaze, and it hit

me at that moment how much the three of them had come to mean to me. They were Evren's friends, his advisors, and comrades, but they had also become mine.

"We should hide her." Queen Veda looked to Evren. "She would be so much safer if we did so."

"No." Evren's magic surged, and I could feel it along with my own. "Gavril already knows that she's with me. There is no use in hiding her now."

"But she would be safer." She looked to Sorin then back to my mate. "We all know that she is the key to the prophecy and keeping her hidden would be the best plan for keeping her out of Gavril's hands."

"I won't hide." I pressed my boots firmly against the floor as I looked around the table. "The prophecy has made it clear that I will be used by one kingdom or another, but I won't be used by hiding. If I'm to help your kingdom then I am to become a weapon."

Queen Veda shook her head, and I knew that she didn't agree but it wasn't her decision to make. Evren said that I was to stay at his side, and for me, that meant even when his brother arrived.

"Sorin and Jorah, make sure that our men are ready." Evren issued the command without looking back at his mother. "We should be prepared for any kind of trick that Gavril could throw our way."

Sorin and Jorah stood, both bowing their heads slightly in Evren's direction before leaving the table.

"Thalia, I'd like for you to work with Adara in my room. Make sure she's ready to control all of her magic if the need arises." He didn't look at me as he gave her his command.

"Of course." Thalia stood and looked to me, but I wasn't ready to leave his side.

"But…" I tugged on Evren's hand, and he lifted them and pressed my knuckles against his mouth once more.

"I will meet you shortly." His gaze never fell from mine. "Stay with Thalia."

I stood slowly, even though it was the last thing I wanted to do, and my magic reached out for Evren as if it was begging me not to leave. I leaned down and grasped his face in my hands, and I pressed my lips to his before I could think better of it. I kissed him hard and desperately. I didn't care that there were still so many in the room watching us. I didn't care that his mother sat next to him while I desperately clung to my mate.

He pressed his forehead to mine as we broke the kiss, and his breath rushed out against my lips. "You are mine," he whispered only loud enough for me to hear, but the possession snaked through every inch of me.

"I am yours." I stood before I could no longer find the will to do so and looked toward Thalia.

She nodded to me once before I followed her from the throne room with the sound of the queen's murmured voice echoing behind us. We pushed through the doors and stepped into the hall, and I took a deep breath that didn't seem to fill my lungs.

"This way." Thalia led me down the hall but not in the direction of mine or Evren's rooms. She took me toward the side of the castle I had never been, and I followed behind her dutifully.

"Where are we going?" I struggled to keep up with her long strides. "I thought Evren wanted us to go back to his room."

Thalia's gaze bounced down the hallway before looking back at me. "Evren is careful with his words, but you and I are going to the library."

"The library? I thought he wanted me to train." I feared that I would have to use my magic when Gavril became a direct threat, and I wasn't sure I was ready.

"He wants us to research the prophecy to find out whatever we can." She wrapped her arm in mine and pulled me closer to her. "He wants to have every advantage possible when Gavril arrives at our door."

"And that advantage lies in the library?"

"Evren knows that power lies in knowledge. Even if we aren't able to find the answer we seek, we may find the answer we don't know we need."

We turned right and went down another long hallway until we reached an ornate set of double doors. Thalia pushed inside and grabbed a small lantern from the table. The library was dark and smelled of old parchment and wood.

It was much bigger than the library I had visited in the fae palace, and I ran my fingers along the spines of the books as we passed.

Thalia led us down the aisles of books, and I followed her step for step as I had no idea where I was going.

"Here." She set the lantern on a small table that faced an old wooden bookshelf filled to the brim with leather-bound books. "This is where we'll start."

I pulled a book from the shelf, dark green leather supple against my fingers, and I sat down at the table and began flipping through it.

It spoke of old fae legends. Legends I had never heard before. There were depictions of former fae kings, and the sacrifices they had made for their people. But it also spoke of power and a thirst for it that had become insatiable. The fae and the vampyres once lived side by side without a single thought of being enemies, but that greed had changed everything.

I quickly flipped through the pages as I found nothing of any use, and then tucked the book back into the shelf. Thalia had three different books laid before her, and she was quickly scanning over them.

I grabbed another book from the shelf and climbed up on the table and set it in my lap. I turned it open, and it landed somewhere in the middle, my attention snagged on a picture of a young Starblessed.

The text spoke of the first Starblessed that was ever noted in our history, a young girl by the name of Alyce, and the humans had feared her for the curse that laid upon her skin. She had been cast out, cast into the woods where the fae and the vampyres lied, and they had referred to her as the Stardoomed. Doomed by the stars, doomed by fate.

The young girl had been taken in by an elderly woman of fae descent, and she raised the girl as if she was her own. The text told of how the girl had been stolen by a vampyre, his thirst rampant and uncontrollable. He had taken from the Stardoomed. Fed from her for only a moment, but the taste of her blood on his lips had almost made him mad with power.

It was the first time either vampyre or fae had seen the power a Starblessed's blood could hold. That power could be used as a weapon. Starblessed were hunted from the human lands and beyond, and legends of how vampyres and fae snatched humans from the world spiraled into the stories that were told today.

I looked up from the book and stared at Thalia. She was still deep in her reading

"Were your parents Starblessed?"

Thalia's gaze jumped up to meet mine, and she slowly shook her head. "I don't remember much of my parents, but I know that neither were blessed by the stars."

"So what? We're just chosen at random? There's no rhyme or reason as to why some of us are Starblessed and others aren't?"

Thalia closed the book in front of her and turned to face me fully. "I read once that stars chose who to bless because they could see your fate before you were even in your mother's womb."

I scoffed. "And you believe that?"

Thalia shrugged and searched my gaze. "I don't know what I believe. All I know is that the blood that runs in our veins has been blessed or cursed, however you want to look at it, and the blood that runs in yours can be our salvation or our damning. Evren is your mate. I know you can feel that down to your bones, and it's hard not to believe in some sort of fate when destiny like him waits for you."

My chest tightened, and she was right. I was destined for him and him for me. "And what of you? What is your destiny?"

"I don't know." She looked back to the book that lay on the table in front of her. "I was taken from my parents at a young age, and I knew very little of my destiny other than I was to belong to Gavril. It hadn't occurred to me that it wasn't the truth until Evren took me from there." She took a deep breath, and I tried not to think about the memories I worried were bombarding her. "Take a look around, Adara. If I am destined for anything, it is to live a life defending my friends, fighting for those that I love. I can't imagine that I wasn't destined for this."

"And Sorin?"

Her back straightened and for a small moment, her face fell. "What of him?"

"Do you believe that he is your fate as well?"

"Sorin deserves a lifetime of blessings, and that isn't something I can give him. Everything I had to offer has already been taken from me, Adara."

I shook my head, but she continued.

"Sorin is fun, but the two of us will never be."

"I don't think he realizes that."

"He does." She stood and placed one of the books back on its shelf. "Sorin knows far more about me than I ever intended him to."

"And you hate that?" I asked.

"Of course, I do." She trailed her fingers over the books, and I wondered what she was looking for. "Like I said before, knowledge is power."

I looked down at the book in front of me as I thought about her words. She was right. Knowledge was power, and fear consumed me as I thought about my own lack of knowing who I was.

My chest ached as I thought of my father. I was equal parts him and my mother, but the only parts of him I knew were due to seeing them through me. My stubbornness, my fight… I knew those didn't come from my mother, and I could only assume I got them from him.

"In that other book you gave me…" I closed the book in front of me and looked back up at Thalia. "It talked about Starblessed being able to amplify their power through nature, to pull from their own supply of power somehow."

Thalia turned toward me and leaned back against the shelf. "I have read of it, but I've never seen it done. It makes sense, though." Her gaze dropped to her feet. "Our magic is like a well. If we use too much of it, we can drain it completely. Only rest and time can refill that well, but I've read that in great times of need, Starblessed have garnered strength from elsewhere."

"Have you ever emptied your power?"

She hesitated for a long moment and clenched her jaw as she spoke. "Only once."

"With Gavril?"

Her gaze snapped up to meet mine, and she pressed a trembling hand against her neck. "Gavril was never strong enough to completely drain me, although he tried many times."

A heaviness settled into my chest as I listened to her without muttering a sound.

"There was once when he came close. It was right before I got out." She absently toyed with the edge of her shirt as her eyes glazed over with the memory. "When they took me back to my cell, I could feel bone-deep tiredness in me, but I was so angry. I shot what was left of my power out of me, and I didn't care where it went. I just wanted to get rid of it for a moment. I wanted to rid myself of the thing Gavril wanted most, and I did."

She swallowed hard, and her gaze met mine again.

"The guards ran from the room in panic as my magic bolted toward them. I was prepared from them to go after Gavril, for

him to come back in fury, but it wasn't him. They went after
their captain, and Evren was the only one who was willing to
come in my cell. I can still remember the taste of the guard's fear
as they scrambled, but there was no fear in Evren's eyes."

My heart ached as I watched my friend relive her hell. I
knew nothing of what she had been through. I had been spared
by Evren before I ever knew of the horrors she remembered.

"I was prepared to fight Evren, hand to hand if I had to until
my magic returned, and he knew it. He reached out for me, and I
somehow managed to knock him on his ass. It wasn't until that
moment that I realized he was going to help get me out."

"And you've not seen Gavril since?"

"No." She crossed her arms over her chest. "It is my understanding that he believes me to be dead."

"Then maybe you should stay out of sight when he arrives.
Let him continue on with that belief."

"No." She shook her head firmly. "Just like you, I won't
hide. I want to look him in the face and see his reaction when he
realizes that I not only escaped him but how highly his brother
regards me."

Pride bloomed in my chest as I stared at her. She had become
my friend in the short time I had been in the Blood kingdom, but
she felt like so much more than that.

There was a soft knock behind me, and a chill ran down my
marks as I turned around to find Evren standing near the long
aisle Thalia had led us down.

"Hi." I swallowed hard as I stared at him and watched a soft
smile form on his lips.

"Hi, princess."

My breath caught in my throat, and the pull he had on me
almost made me forget that Thalia was in the room until I heard
her move behind me.

"Any changes?" She moved to my side and pressed her
hands onto the table.

"No." He shook his head softly. "My brother and his men should be here by midmorning tomorrow." His gaze flicked back and forth between us. "We should all get some rest before he does."

"Of course." Thalia reached forward and squeezed my hand in hers for only a moment before she passed me and made her way toward Evren. "I'll be ready."

"I know you will." He nodded toward her as she went to pass, but he caught her arm in his hand before she could. She looked up at him, but her gaze didn't meet his. He pulled her toward him and wrapped his arms around her as he pulled her into his chest.

Her body seemed to sag against him, and I couldn't imagine the thoughts that were clouding her mind. She allowed herself only a moment before she pulled herself away from him and ran her hand down the back of her neck.

"You'll wake me if anything changes?"

"Of course." He nodded once before his gaze landed on me.

Thalia pushed through the door of the library, and I wondered if she would seek out Sorin. Despite the words she said, I knew that she found some sort of solace in him, and I couldn't imagine a time that she would need it more.

"We should get some rest as well." Evren moved toward me and didn't stop until he rounded the table and pressed himself between my knees. His hands cupped my cheeks as I looked up at him, and he searched my face as his breath rushed out of him.

"Are you okay?" I swallowed and sat the book I still held to my side.

"It would be foolish for me not to be fearful, princess. My brother is coming, and I know without a doubt that you're the thing he wants."

"But you won't let him have me." There was no question to my words.

"No, princess. You are mine."

NINETEEN

E vren held my hand in his, and he held me as close to him as I could get until we finally reached the door to his room. The loud click of it closing behind us echoed throughout his room and in my chest.

My hand trembled in his, and I couldn't get the restlessness to leave my body no matter how badly I begged it to. Tomorrow was coming, and I wasn't ready to face it.

Not yet.

But I had no choice.

A black gown hung near Evren's bed, and he nodded toward it as he led me farther in the room.

"That's for tomorrow." His voice was gruff and filled with his own emotion. "When Gavril arrives, you will be the last to enter the throne room. You will be presented as my betrothed before him."

"Okay." I nodded even as my chest tightened.

"But I don't want you to go anywhere near him. Once you enter, you come straight to me." He practically growled the words. "I want you at my side the entire time."

"Okay." My lips trembled and my breath shook in my chest.

He turned back toward me, his eyes assessing and dark. "I won't let him touch you, Adara. He will not take you from me."

I nodded even as I felt fear eat at my chest. I didn't want to be in the same kingdom as Gavril, let alone the same room. I trusted Evren, but my mistrust of his brother was stronger.

"Princess." Evren pulled his hand from mine and pressed it against my chin. He lifted until I was forced to look at him. "You are my mate, and I will not allow him any more of you than he's already taken."

"What if he gives you no choice?" I searched his dark gaze even as his eyes narrowed.

"There is no way for him to force my hand where I won't pick you. You are my choice, Adara. In any question, under any circumstance, I will choose you."

I gasped as I tried to pull in a breath, and Evren's hand snaked around to the back of my neck. His fingers tangled in my hair and gripped almost to the point of pain.

"You are mine, Adara, and I am yours. No one has the power to change that. Not even us." His lips pressed against mine, and he kissed me slowly. He kissed me as if he was trying to memorize every inch of my lips, every dip and curve.

He backed us up until the backs of my thighs hit his bed, and he slowly lowered me and pressed his knee between my legs.

"I thought we needed rest." I smiled against his lips and pressed my thighs into his hips.

"We do." He nodded and ran his mouth along my jaw. He took his time kissing the sensitive skin along my neck until his teeth nipped at my earlobe. "But gods, I need you more."

He stood, taking a step back from me, and started slowly unbuttoning his dark shirt. "I have been able to think of little else since you climbed out of my bed this morning."

He pulled his shirt from his trousers, and I sat up and slowly pulled my own boot from my foot. I let it slide to the floor in a loud thump, and my heart rate skyrocketed with every second that passed between us.

I pushed off my other boot before moving my trembling fingers to my shirt. Evren stood before me, bare from the waist up, and he slowly undid his trousers before lowering them down his hips.

I could hardly catch my breath as I watched him kick his trousers behind him or as I pulled my own shirt over my head.

"You are so perfect." His hand gripped my calf, and his fingers crept up it until he reached the back of my knee. He jerked it forward, knocking me back onto my back, and his hand continued it's path up my leg. He pressed both of my legs between his thighs, holding them in place, and he moved up my thigh at a painfully slow pace. My chest rose and fell harshly as I tried to anticipate his next move.

He was so beautiful standing in front of me. He was completely bare, not a single part of him hidden, and it hit me more than ever that this man who was half fae and half vampyre, every part of him was meant for me. He was my mate, and there wasn't a single part of me that doubted that truth.

His hand grazed over my sex, barely applying any pressure, but I jumped under his touch and tried to clamp my legs together. A smirk marred his face as he finally reached the top of my trousers and slowly unlaced them.

His hands moved to my hips, and he tugged the leather down my hips and below my ass as he stared down at me. "So beautiful."

He leaned forward and his breath rushed out against my sex. I pressed my hand to my mouth and bit down on my palm as I tried to force myself not to beg him for more.

He pressed his mouth to my hip bone before slowly running his nose along the length of my hips until he reached the other. He looked up at me as his tongue peeked out from his lips and traced along my skin. I thought it was enough to kill me, this torture he was putting me through, but then his teeth grazed against my sensitive skin and my back arched from the bed.

I could feel moisture pooling between my thighs, begging both me and him for release, and I tried to clamp my thighs together to relieve some of the pressure that was building there.

I was drowning in my want for him, suffocating on my need.

And he was taking his time as he tormented me with my lust.

I squirmed between him, but my legs were still trapped between his and he paid me no mind as he slowly made his way toward my sex.

"Please." The plea fell from my lips, and I lifted my own hand to squeeze my breast. "Oh gods."

"Tell me what you want." His breath whispered over my sex, and I whimpered. "I will give you anything you ask of me." He murmured the words just before his tongue pushed through my slit.

I bowed off the bed and reached down and tangled my hand in his hair. I held him against me, desperate for him not to leave, and he growled against my sex before he began eating at my flesh with ferocity.

He reached below me and gripped my bottom in his hands, and he lifted me off the bed and more firmly against his mouth. My legs were still pinned together, but somehow it only intensified what he was doing. He sucked my nub into his mouth, and I cried out as pleasure crashed into me in a wave.

"The smell of you," he growled as he lifted his gaze to meet mine. "The smell of your desire for me, it has become as vital to me as breathing. I would starve without the taste of you."

"Evren."

He lifted and took a step back from me before he ripped my trousers off me completely.

My thighs were slick with my want for him, and I tried to hide my shame as he pushed my legs apart and knelt on the bed between them. He ran his hand through the moisture that lied there with a moan on his lips before lifting his fingers to my lips.

"Taste it, princess. Taste what no other man will ever get from you."

I wrapped my lips around his fingers and pressed my tongue to the tips as he watched me.

"Tell me you're mine, Adara." He pulled his fingers from my mouth and slowly ran them down my neck and onto my chest.

"I am yours."

His eyes closed as if my words were intoxicating, and he gripped my thigh in his hand and lifted it until it pressed against his hip.

"No one can change that." He looked back to me as he ran his length through my sex and caused me to squirm beneath him. He was looking at me like no one ever had before, and I didn't know if it was that or the way he was touching me that made me feel like I would never come back from this desperation inside me. "No matter what happens tomorrow. You are mine, and I am yours."

I nodded just as he pushed inside of me and stole the breath from my lips.

"You are my mate." He thrust into me, and his chest came down against mine. His lips met mine, and he kissed me as he began moving inside me. "You are to be my wife, Adara. You are everything to me."

"As you are to me." I gripped my fingers in his hair and moved my hips beneath him. "You are all that I need, Evren. All that I want."

He groaned against my mouth, and his hips slammed harder against me. I could feel it rising inside me, that pleasure that only he could give me, and when he ran his fingers along my ribs, I couldn't stop the tremor that coursed through my body.

His teeth grazed over my neck, and my hips surged off the bed.

"When the threat of my brother is gone…" He moved his mouth over my collarbone, and I whimpered as I felt his teeth nip there. "I plan to do nothing but discover everything that makes you fall apart. I will spend days getting to know your body in a way that not even you can fathom."

"Evren." I clamped my eyes closed and pressed my head into the bed. It was climbing inside of me, and I felt like I was going to fall apart. Every part of me was fracturing, splintering in my need, and he was the only cure.

His lips pressed against my chest once more before he sat back onto his knees and gripped my hip in his hand. He didn't stop moving inside me, and I cried out as his thumb brushed over my nub.

"Give it to me, princess." He growled. "Let me have every part of you."

I didn't stand a chance of denying him. My body hummed under his command, and that dam inside of me broke lose as the pleasure he drew from my body came crashing through. He pressed his palm at the edge of my lower stomach, just before my sex, and he thrust into me hard.

I cried out and dug my fingers into his bedding. It was too much, the pleasure crashing into me, and I feared I would break, but Evren held me beneath him as he thrust into me one last time and found his own release.

He fell forward, his forehead pressing against my stomach, and neither of us spoke as we tried to catch our breath.

We stayed like that for a long moment before Evren pulled himself from my body and laid beside me. He pulled me toward him until my upper half was laying across his chest, and he kissed me lazily as the aftershocks still coursed through my body.

"Get some rest, princess. Tomorrow will come whether we want it to or not."

TWENTY

I wiped my sweating hands down the sides of my glittering black gown. The dress was provocative, a statement I was sure that my mate was trying to make. The neckline was deep and stopped just below the edge of my breastbone.

A simple string of diamonds fell against the base of my neck and drew attention there if you weren't already drawn to the long slit that reached the top of my right thigh.

I was Evren's mate, dripping in a black dress that looked so like him, like us, and I knew he wanted his brother to see that.

But my back was completely covered. Every bit of my mark was touched by fabric and shielded from everyone else's eyes. The only marks they could see were those that lay along my cheeks. The rest were hidden, and it wasn't because Evren wanted Gavril to know my power belonged to him.

But because it belonged to me.

My mark wasn't a spectacle here, a damn trophy to be showed off. I was more than that, and Evren was making that clear.

The doors to the throne room opened, and a soft hush fell over the room as I stepped through. Gavril and his men stood at the base of Evren's throne, but I didn't dare look in his direction. I was too busy staring ahead at my mate who was watching my every move.

He tracked every step like a hunter waiting to strike, and even in a room full of people, my stomach dipped from the look in his eyes.

I could feel the others' eyes on me as well, including Gavril's, as I made my way toward him. The queen wasn't in the room. Another power play from Evren. He was in charge here, and he wanted Gavril to know that.

He was his brother, but Evren was set to rule. And he would do so without fear of his brother.

My gaze fell on Jorah and Sorin who both stood at the base of the dais. Neither one were standing between Evren and Gavril, a clear stance that their prince didn't need protection, but in unity.

But it was Thalia who took my breath away. She wore a deep blue dress that made her look like a goddess, and she stood at Evren's side. Not a single step below him, perfectly even. And every bit of her scars were on full display, and I knew she did that purposefully.

She wanted Gavril to remember what he did. To see her scars and remember exactly what he had taken from her. But Evren wouldn't allow that memory to be standing at the base of the dais.

He honored her at his side. Gavril took from her, but Evren held her in the highest esteem.

I looked to the empty throne next to Evren, the seat where he had asked me to sit, and Sorin held out his hand as I lifted my foot to take my first step upon the dais. I took it without question and let him help me to the top before he dipped into a small bow.

Sorin's honor in front of these people had my throat feeling tight. I looked to the throne then back to my mate. He was sitting back on his throne, still watching me meticulously, and he looked so unbothered by his brother being here. But I knew the truth.

So I did the only thing I could. I stepped forward, not toward the throne that was waiting for me, but toward him. I dipped down until my hands were resting on either side of him, and I brought my face close to his.

He was their prince, the man who would rule this kingdom, but he was so much more to me. And while Evren had his own points to get across to his brother, so did I.

I leaned forward until our noses were almost touching, and my stomach dipped when Evren's lips formed into a smirk and he ran his tongue across them.

"You're meant to be sitting over there, princess." He spoke softly for only me to hear as he cocked his head to the side where the throne waited for me.

"That's what I'm told." I lifted my right hand and ran it across his cleanly shaven jaw. "But I rarely do as I'm told."

He didn't have time to respond because I closed the space between us and pressed my lips to his. It didn't matter that we were being watched and everyone was calculating our every move. This was about far more than any of them.

I chose Evren in this lifetime, and I would in the next. And he needed to know that truth.

I pulled back, but only far enough so I could turn, and I sat upon his right knee as I finally faced Gavril for the first time since I entered the room.

Evren's hand snaked around my hip, and he pressed it to my lower stomach before he pulled me back against him possessively. My back, my mark, was pressed against his chest, and he didn't hesitate to keep his hand exactly where it was.

"Brother, you do remember Adara, don't you?" Evren's fingers skimmed along my belly, causing me to squirm in his lap even as I looked at his brother.

The anger on Gavril's face was palpable even though he tried to mask it. "Of course." He gently nodded in my direction. "She does look quite good on your arm as a whore, but you should remember that she was born to be a queen."

I stiffened, as did Evren, and I could feel his power rolling beneath me.

"You should watch your words when you're speaking about my betrothed." Evren lifted my left hand in his and pressed a gentle kiss along my finger that would soon hold his ring.

That barely-veiled mask slipped from Gavril's face. "Well, it is my future queen that I have come to discuss." His hand rested against the hilt of his sword, and my eyes tracked the movement. "You taking her from me was even more treasonous than you taking the other Starblessed that stands at your side. They both belonged to me."

"Neither belong to you," Evren growled from behind me, and his chest pressed firmer against my back. "You threw Thalia away like she was trash you were finished using."

My gaze slid to Sorin, and even before my eyes landed on his handsome face, I could feel his fury radiating from him in waves. He would kill the crowned prince for his offense to Thalia and that alone.

"And the Starblessed?" Gavril nodded in my direction as if I was an object to discuss. "I wasn't quite finished using her. But I take it by the way she's clinging to your leg like a bitch in heat that she is no longer pure."

Evren's magic shot out around me, swallowing me in his darkness, and Gavril laughed. This was exactly what he wanted. He was pushing Evren's buttons for a reason, and I didn't realize why until I felt another source of magic slam into me.

My gaze met Gavril's, and he cocked his head as he smiled at me. His power felt strong, and for a moment, fear raced through me as I stared into his hollow eyes.

"Don't worry, brother. I won't snatch the Starblessed out of your hands like you did me. I will let her choose her fate."

Evren's hands tightened around me and pulled me impossibly closer to him.

"Did you know, Starblessed? That your blood has a really particular taste." Gavril ran his fingers along his lips as if he was remembering the moment he took from me. "The moment it touched my lips, I knew that I had tasted it before."

I didn't say a word, but my back straightened and the marks burned against my skin.

"What do you want, Gavril?" Evren growled through his teeth, and his magic rumbled around me.

"What is mine." He nodded in my direction before taking a step toward me. "I am to rule with her at my side."

Thalia shifted closer to me, and I could feel her magic coming to life beneath her skin.

Gavril noticed her too. He looked toward her before that same smirk crossed his lips. "Are you going to protect her, Thalia? You couldn't protect yourself."

Rage like I had never felt before came over me, and I stood from Evren's lap before he could stop me. My magic shot from my fingers and swirled around me as I stared at the prince to whom I was promised.

"You will never speak to her again." I hardly recognized my voice, but I heard the gasps of others around us. This wasn't a part of the plan, to show Gavril the amount of power I held, but it refused to lay dormant while he spoke to her like that. "You do so again, and you will rule nothing."

Every part of my skin felt alive with my power, but I could still feel Evren's wrapping around me, protecting me even when I wasn't sure I needed it.

"So this is why you took her?" Gavril's gaze darkened as he took me in, and I could practically see his plotting turning in his mind. "They say you are Father's selfless son, but look at you taking all the power for yourself."

"I don't want her for her power." Evren's hand wrapped

around my thigh and pulled me back a step until I was standing between his legs.

"Lie to the girl all you want, brother, but we both know exactly what you want from her."

Gavril turned and looked behind him and nodded someone forward. One of his soldiers, a man I recognized from the fae palace, stepped forward with his hand wrapped around the arm of another. The person had a hood covering their face, and the moon pendant around my neck burned against my skin.

He shoved the person forward until they fell to their knees in front near Gavril, and he reached forward and tugged the hood back from their head.

I didn't recognize the man before me, but my power seemed to. It snaked around me as if it were ready for anything, but both me and my power couldn't look away from the man.

"What is this?" I shook my head and reached up to rub the spot where my pendant lay.

"Ask your betrothed." Gavril nodded behind me. "I'm most certain he will remember him."

The man looked up at me, and there was so much sadness in his eyes. His hair was brown, a similar shade to my own, and his eyes were bright. But it was the star mark along the top of his hand that held my attention.

"Who is this?" I asked again, my voice firmer and full of power.

Evren stood and pressed his chest to my back, and I could feel his rough rush of breath against the back of my neck.

"It's odd, don't you think?" Gavril ran his hand over his jaw. "That you wouldn't recognize your own father."

I jerked backward and slammed into Evren. His hand wrapped around my middle and his power snaked around every other inch of me.

I shook my head as I stared at the man I had no recollection of. "You're lying."

"Am I?" Gavril chuckled and pulled on the man's hair until he was forced to stand again. "How do you think I recognize the taste of your blood, Adara?" He lifted the man's wrist in his hand and showed me the scars that lay there. "I have fed from your father's blood for years while I waited for you. He had refused me your hand in marriage so I took it against his will."

"My father is dead." My voice trembled, and I studied the man's face. I didn't know him, but I was a fool if I tried to deny that there were so many similarities staring back at me. "My father wasn't a Starblessed."

Gavril chuckled again, and the sound made my magic surge. "It's sad how little you really know. How easily you were kept in the dark. Isn't it, Evren?"

My chest tightened, and I looked over my shoulder at my mate.

"He didn't tell you?" Gavril was still speaking, but I couldn't pull my attention away from Evren. "He was the one who captured your father after he refused to give us you. Evren is the one who hand-delivered your father to our queen."

Evren's gaze searched mine, and even though he didn't say a word, his eyes softened, begging for forgiveness. Gavril was telling the truth.

I jerked out of Evren's hold and almost fell forward. Thalia moved to my side as Gavril laughed.

"Tell me that isn't true." I stared at my mate, and I wanted him to say it even though I could already feel the truth in my bones.

I wanted him to destroy the feeling that was clawing at my chest and prove to me that he was nothing like his brother.

"It's not what you think." Evren reached out for me, but I took another step back. "I had no idea your father was alive."

"But you're the one who took him?" The words slipped past my lips like an accusation, and I didn't want it to be true.

My chest ached as I stared at him and willed him to tell me anything other than what I feared.

"I did." Evren swallowed hard. "But I had no idea what it would lead to." He motioned to my father. "I did it because Queen Kaida had ordered it so. The same way she had ordered me to deliver you to her kingdom."

"And you did so dutifully." My words were laced with anger, but I couldn't stop them. It didn't matter that Evren hadn't known me then. He had taken my father from me. He had delivered him to my enemy, and I couldn't stop the pain that sliced through my chest at the thought.

"Princess," Evren whispered my name, but my gaze snapped to Gavril as he cleared his throat.

"I offer a life for a life, Adara." He crossed his arms and the smug look on his face ate at me. "If you want your father to live, then you will come with me."

"That's not fucking happening." Evren's growl boomed through the throne room, and he stepped forward to block me from Gavril. "Adara will go nowhere with you."

"Then would you like the honor of killing her father?" Gavril pulled his sword from his scabbard and held it toward Evren.

Everyone reacted, weapons drawn and emotions tense. Sorin and Jorah moved to my side ready to defend me and Thalia with any means necessary.

"You are the one who took him from her the first time. Maybe you should be the one to take him from her for eternity."

I let my gaze slide to the man at Gavril's side, and I stared at this man who I should have recognized immediately. I had dreamed of him constantly. Prayed for a day when I would remember his face, but it was nothing like I imagined.

His lips held the same curve as mine, and his eyes were the same shade of ice blue that everyone told me my own had reminded them of. The eye that matched my father.

This man that stood before me was a stranger, but when I

looked into his eyes, something felt familiar. It felt like a home that I never had, a home that I had always been searching for.

A home I had thought I found in Evren.

"I'll do it." I didn't let my gaze fall from his even as he shook his head.

"Please, no." His voice was gruff and full of age, years that I never got to experience with him.

"I won't let them take you from me again." I spoke only to my father, and I didn't care who heard me.

"You're not taking her." Evren's magic swirled around his hands, and I could feel his fury without looking at him. "I will destroy your entire kingdom before I allow you to take her again."

"And you believe she will still choose you?" Gavril stared at his brother even as he pulled my father closer to him. "You're going to let her father die, and you think she'll still choose you?"

"Don't touch him." I stepped forward and my magic shot out of my fingers. It was moments away from slamming into Gavril before he blocked it with his own.

"Be careful, Starblessed." The smile fell from his lips, and his hand tightened around my father. "Don't do something you will regret for the rest of your life."

He lifted his hand with his sword and brought it close to my father's chest.

"I'm sorry, Adara." My father's words were a plea on his lips. "I'm sorry for everything."

"No." I held out my hands and tears welled in my eyes. "You want a trade, and I said I'll do it."

I took another step closer to him, and Evren's magic wrapped tighter around me. I looked over to my mate, and all I could see was his anger and pain.

"I won't let you do this, Adara."

"You don't have a choice." I shook my head and guilt slammed into me as I watched the way his face crumpled. I was so angry at him for the things he had done, but I was angrier about the fact that he hadn't told me.

He was my mate, and I had chosen him, but he had left me in the dark.

Evren quickly moved in front of me and moved down the dais toward his brother. Gavril stiffened and his hand tightened around his sword.

"Let her father go." His voice was the command of a ruler. This was the crowned prince that was meant to be. "You want a trade and you'll have one, but you will not take her."

"What?" My stomach tightened, and Thalia called out his name.

"Let her father go, and I will go with you willingly."

"I need her to fulfill the prophecy." Gavril nodded toward me.

"One will defeat, one will cower." Evren recited part of the prophecy aloud for us all to hear. "I will go willingly as your prisoner. I will cower to you in order to save her. It is her fate that will begin your rule."

Gavril stared at his brother for a long time before he looked up at me, and I couldn't quit thinking about what Sorin had once told me. Queen Kaida needed my hand or Evren's head.

"No." I shook my head and tried to move forward, but Evren's magic slammed into me like a wall. "No!"

Evren held out his hand toward his brother and black magic trailed from his fingers. "You let her father go, she remains in the safety of the Blood kingdom, and I will go with you without a fight."

Gavril looked down at his hand before he slowly lowered the sword from my father, and I could hardly see as tears began trailing down my face.

"No, Evren!" I shot my magic into his, but it hardly made a difference.

"You said a life for a life." Evren was completely ignoring

me as he spoke to his brother. "I am the crowned prince of the Blood kingdom. Take my life for his."

I searched for Sorin and Jorah, and I could see the panic in their eyes. I hurried toward them and wrapped my hands around Sorin's arms.

"Stop him," I begged, and Sorin looked down at me with pity filling his gaze. "Do not let him do this, Sorin."

"I made a promise to him." Sorin reached forward and wiped the moisture from my face. "I will protect you no matter the cost."

"Swear it," Gavril held out his hand toward Evren, and I could feel his own magic radiating from his skin even though I couldn't see it. There wasn't a single visible sign of his magic. "Swear it, and I'll let him go."

I moved out of Sorin's touch and looked for my friend. "Thalia!"

A deal sealed in magic couldn't simply be undone. If Evren took his hand, if he swore to his brother while his magic sealed his words, there would be nothing we could do.

Thalia's panicked gaze slammed into mine, and her bright blue magic slipped through her fingers as she tried to penetrate the wall that Evren's magic was holding up. She was blocked as easily as I had been, and I watched in horror as Gavril took Evren's hand in his.

"I swear." Evren's magic wrapped around Gavril's wrist, and I could feel their magic mixing together as their deal began sealing between the two of them. My chest felt like it was caving in as I watched them. My magic swelled inside of me as I made my decision.

They spoke of me as if I was the key to saving their kingdom, but they were wrong. It wasn't me this world needed. It was him.

It always had been.

I gathered every bit of my power I could before letting it

pour from my fingers in a wave of magic. It shot into Evren's magic and bent to my will. I didn't stop until my power hit him full force.

It shot into him when he wasn't expecting it and knocked him away from his brother. His hand fell from Gavril's before either could seal with their magic between them, and Evren's gaze shot to mine.

There was confusion and panic staring back at me, but I didn't stop. I moved toward him as I pushed my power harder, and Evren hit the ground as my black inky magic poured from me and slammed into him.

"You will take me." I looked up at Gavril, and I could see the shock in his own eyes. "Swear that you will take me instead of him, and I will go with you willingly. I am the key to the prophecy. Not him. He is not to be harmed."

He looked back and forth between his brother and me, and he knew the truth of my words. Taking his brother wouldn't get him me. It wouldn't give him what he truly wanted.

He would have nothing but a dead brother and a betrothed he was still unable to touch.

"I swear it." He nodded once, and I sent a trickle of my magic in his direction.

He watched every move it made as it wrapped around his hand and wrist, and I kept my magic pushed hard against Evren.

Gavril's magic mixed with my own, and he nodded once. I could feel it lock into place, the deal between us, and I could barely hear Evren as he screamed out my name.

I looked back at him and slammed my magic harder and harder until he stopped fighting against me. Then I pushed harder. I forced my magic into him until I feared that it would be too much.

I had no idea what I was doing, but I remembered what he told me. We were mates which meant our magic was linked. He had said that it was legend that one mate could pull from another, and I didn't have time to figure out how it worked. I poured my magic into him harder and harder until I could feel it draining from me.

Evren shook his head, but he couldn't stop me. Not now. Not when so much of my magic was already pouring into him. I felt it the moment he opened up, the moment he accepted what I gave him, and I didn't stop until I could feel myself draining fully.

"I thought you wanted him unharmed." Gavril laughed as he wrapped his fingers around my bicep and tugged me into his side. "It looks like you're going to do the job for me, Starblessed."

I knew how it looked. My magic was still slamming into Evren, and even as my gaze slid past him to Thalia, I could see the fear in her eyes. But none of them had the power to stop me.

Her blue magic hit my own, not to harm me, but to stop me from harming her prince, but it did no good.

I would go with Gavril willingly, but I would play no part in his plan. When he took me, he would be taking me without my powers. He would be taking a Starblessed that held no blessings to make his prophecy come true.

I could feel the bottom of the well, every but of my magic drained from me, and I sagged against Gavril as the last of my magic trailed from my fingers.

The throne room was eerily quiet as Evren took a deep breath and shook his head. "Please don't do this, princess."

"It's already done." Gavril laughed with his mouth near my ear. "You gave yourself up for a man you think you love." Gavril pressed against my neck, and I tried to jerk away from him but I was so tired.

Evren climbed to his feet with fury in his eyes, but Gavril lifted his blade to my neck just as Evren took a step in our direction.

"He craves your blood as much as I do, Adara. He craves your power. You are nothing more to him than a pawn."

"I am his mate." My words were as weak as I felt, but I hoped Evren could hear the truth behind them. I hoped he knew what they meant.

"Mate," Gavril spat out the word, and his hands tightened against me. "Do you think fate knew he was your mate when my mother ordered him to take your father from you? Was that fate or his own power that caused him to lock your father in the dungeon and guarantee that your own blood would never get in the way of you being his? You may hate me, Starblessed, but the man you just saved is no better than I. He is worse. He damned you to this life. He damned you to be mine even though it's the last thing he could want."

I didn't believe him. Evren may have been the one to take my father to the Fae kingdom, but I couldn't bring myself to believe he knew my father was still alive.

I couldn't bring myself to believe that he would ever do such a thing to me.

"Get your fucking hands off her, Gavril," Evren growled, and Gavril's thumb rubbed along my neck right where Evren could see.

"So possessive over something that doesn't belong to him," Gavril murmured before running his nose along my skin and breathing me in.

I looked away from Evren as I tried not to cry out, and my gaze hit my father's. My father stood before me, but I still didn't know him. I knew even less about him than I thought I had.

I feared what he had been through as I looked over his aging face. I had been in that castle for weeks, and the entire time he had been there. He had been tortured and feed from just as Thalia had.

"I'm sorry," I mouthed the words to him, and I could see his emotion shutter across his face.

I was so sorry for all of it. For everything he had been through, for the decision I had to make.

Gavril pulled me back toward the door of the throne room, and his men surrounded us. I could feel Evren's magic along with my own, and I looked back to my mate as our dark magic surrounded him.

"I love you, Evren." The words fell from my lips just as Gavril lifted his hand and a magic like I had never felt before consumed me.

Cold, empty darkness ravaged me, and Evren's face was the last thing I saw as I let it take me.

Want more from the Stars and Shadows Series?
A Kingdom of Venom and Vows is coming March 23, 2023.
Preorder now!

THANK YOU

Thank you so much for taking a chance on the Stars and Shadows series. The love you all have shown for this series has blown me away, and I can't wait to bring you the third book and the conclusion to Adara and Evren's story.

I would love for you to join my reader group, Hollywood, so we can connect and talk about all of your thoughts on A Kingdom of Stars and Shadows! This group is the first place to find out about cover reveals, book news, and new releases!

Again, thank you for going on this journey with me.

Xo,

Holly Renee
www.authorhollyrenee.com

Before You Go
Please consider leaving an honest review.

ABOUT THE AUTHOR

USA Today Bestselling Author, Holly Renee brings readers a pinch of angst, an indulgence of heat, and the perfect amount of heart in every book.

Born and raised in East Tennessee, she is a married mom of two wild children. When she's not writing, you can find her reading, pretending to be a dragon for the hundredth time that day, being disgustingly in love with her husband, or chilling in the middle of the lake with her sunglasses and a float.

Holly is a lover of all things romance, Mexican food and yoga pants.

SOCIAL LINKS
authorhollyrenee.com
Instagram: @authorhollyrenee
TikTok: @authorhollyrenee
Facebook Reader Group: Hollywood (Holly Renee's Reader Group)

ALSO BY HOLLY RENEE

Stars and Shadows Series:

A Kingdom of Stars and Shadows

A Kingdom of Blood and Betrayal

The Good Girls Series:

Where Good Girls Go to Die

Where Bad Girls Go to Fall

Where Bad Boys are Ruined

The Boys of Clermont Bay Series:

The Touch of a Villain

The Fall of a God

The Taste of an Enemy

The Deceit of a Devil

The Seduction of Pretty Lies

The Temptation of Dirty Secrets

The Rock Bottom Series:

Trouble with the Guy Next Door

Trouble with the Hotshot Boss

Trouble with the Fake Boyfriend

The Wrong Prince Charming

ACKNOWLEDGMENTS

Thank you to my husband, Hubie. My #1 fan. I would choose you in any lifetime.

Thank you to all the readers and bloggers for taking a chance on this series. I am forever grateful that you chose to spend your time reading this series and constantly in awe of support. Thank you.

Thank you to my entire team who I couldn't do this without. Amanda, Christina, Katie, Ellie, Rumi, Brittni, Cynthia, Tori, and Savannah: thank you, thank you, thank you.

For Rachel Brookes, your support and advice is priceless. Thank you for everything.